A Moment of Joy

Essays on Art, Writing and Life

By

Allison Tzu Yu Lin

· Acknowledgements ·

I am grateful to my colleagues in the Faculty of Education, Gaziantep University. With their friendship, I am able to have this book done. Moreoever, my thanks go to Mr Michael Song, the President of Showwe Publisher in Taipei, Taiwan. With his encouragement, this interdisciplinary book finally comes into its shape. I am also grateful to be helped by Mr T. H. Lin, the chief editor and the acting manager of Showwe publisher. With his suggestion, I can put all chapters together in a book form. Finally, I want to thank my family members. Their love makes me feel that I am actually doing something meaningful through writing.

Tzu Yu Allison Lin
Gaziantep 2014

A Moment of Joy

· Preface ·

The idea of having a collection of essays published is quite a recent one. Right after I joined Education Faculty, about one year ago, it came to my mind. In Turkey, the study of literature is actually quite a problematic one. Students in departments which are related to literary studies (in Faculty of Letters or Faculty of Letters and Sciences) mostly worry about their futures, since the system itself will represent a bit of challenge for them to become language teachers. Any studies related to literature, in general, is not for enjoyment or or fun. The study itself, indeed, expresses a general anxiety of facing a future of uncertainty.

Under such a different, and yet challenging academic environment, it is really difficult to teach literature, especially literature in English. Students are used to be passive. Creative thinkings and links (for example, literature and critical theory, literature and visual arts) are not so much expected as in other countries. Too much links and creative works would be seen as unclear and as something unnecessary.

Teaching and doing research are truly quite different things. In research, I am able to care more about what I can achieve, instead of thinking about what can students achieve in the class. It may look very much impossible, to make students see what I see; still, it is worth it to put those ideas into words. In reading, rather than in listening and taking notes, they can also at least try to appreciate not only literature as literature, arts as arts, but to feel the connection which is beyond words and images.

Tzu Yu Allison Lin
Gaziantep 2014

· Contents ·

v

· Chapter 1 ·

Through the Gaze:
History, Literature and Arts

What is fair in men passes away, but not so in art.
Leonardo Da Vinci, *The Da Vinci Notebooks*

History is somehow consumed in one's own everyday life. I want to demonstrate the way in which 'history' is represented as memory, treated as a critical focus, in order to show the meaning of auto-biographical and biographical writings. I trace the concept of history and memory, to see their functions and meanings in literature and arts, especially in Walter Benjamin's terms. My aim is to define history, and to show it as a methodology in literary studies. Secondly, different forms of literature can be seen as ways of responding to the past. They create new meanings and new aesthetics of history through literary techniques such as flashback, photographic vision and visual impressions.

This summer, on 25 August 2013, I came across to an image in a book. The book is a gift from an old friend, titled *Paintings that Changed the World*. The image *A Baker and His Wife* (Anonymous, Roman, 1st Century AD, in Reichold and Graf 17) caught my eyes, reminding in me the exhibition I failed to see in the British Museum—*Life and Death*. Starring by the couple in the eyes, I strongly feel the way in which Walter Benjamin felt in his critical essay, 'A Short History of Photography'. In the essay, he talked about the aura which the viewer sees in the fish wife's eyes (*Newhaven, Elizabeth Johnstone, The Beautiful Fishwife*. Photo: David Octavius Hill, in Benjamin 9). The gaze of the fish wife and the Roman couple's image of Naples, through the channel of history, immediately come to my present, under my gaze. At the moment of gaze, somehow we realise that they had never been dead.

Madame Lisa del Giocondo is well-known, because she is

the very character of Leonardo Da Vinci's *Mona Lisa* (1503-05, in Reichold and Graf 63). Her face represents an unchallengeable sense of Beauty, representing eternity. Through Madame Lisa's gaze, the viewer can 'be lost in the poetry of her smile', as Angelo Conti claims in his *On Mona Lisa* (qtd. in Reichold and Graf 63). 'The Eye', as Da Vinci called 'the window of the soul' (Da Vinci 93), comes to make a moment of the gaze to eternity. Through her gaze, Beauty and eternity come to state the power of love and memory. A similar experience of the subjective gaze can be reached in Michelangelo's literary works. For instance, in his sonnet XXV,

'Tell me, I beg, Love, if my eyes indeed
See all the truth of beauty which I claim,
Or if I have within me now the same
Power to see all the beauty that I need?

You ought to know the answer since you came
With her to break my peace, disturb my rest.

I would not let the smallest sight be lost
For such a love, nor ask a lesser flame'.

'The beauty that you see is truly hers,
But as it grows it rises higher still
If through the eyes it reaches to the soul.

Here it becomes divine and beautiful,
And on a mortal thing it now confers
An immortality your eyes to fill'. (Buonarroti 49)

Certainly, the conversation between the narrator and Love shows
that Madam Lisa's Beauty is in the eye of the beholder. As long
as the viewer is watching her portrait, she will never die. In
Sigmund Freud's reading, Leonardo's Lisa comes to express
'his most secret mental impulses', which are about his artistic
representations of his childhood memory, 'phantasy' and 'the
intensity of the erotic relations between mother and child' (Freud
107). In other words, Madame Lisa's portrait is Leonardo's

symbolic 'historical writing', showing his 'conscious memory of the events of his maturity' (Freud 84). The mother's 'passionate kiss' on the boy's lips (Freud 107), comes to create the 'mysteriously dream-like' (Freud 108) canvas of *Mona Lisa*, as the childhood memory lingering 'between reserve and seduction, and between the most devoted tenderness and a sensuality that is ruthlessly demanding' (Freud 108).

Childhood memory is significant, in a way which the present moment is lived through the past. The past and the present are like two opposite poles, which synthesis Virginia Woolf's many characters of Mr and Mrs in *Mrs Dalloway's Party*, as they come together to Mrs Dalloway's party in her drawing-room in London. Woolf's verbal images come to depict a historical discourse, as the dialectical moment appears in her characters' thoughts.

As Big Ben strokes at eleven o'clock, Mrs Dalloway feels an air of freshness in the middle of June, 'as if issued to children on a beach' (Woolf 19). Although Clarissa is physically located 'in the murmur of wheels and the shuffle of footsteps', in central London on the street of Westminster, she feels that 'the moment was complete' (Woolf 19), as the memory of her 'happy childhood' comes back to her. The stroke of Big Ben somehow works magically, as 'there is nothing to take the place of childhood. A leaf of mint brings it back: or a cup with a blue ring (Woolf 19).

Memory is central to Proust's work. The process of searching for the 'lost time' seems to bring up the intensity of emotions, effortlessly. The feeling of happiness is in the recognition of the meaning of Marcel's childhood memory. And yet, this 'knowledge' (Szondi 11) also brings a totally opposite feeling—'the frightfully painful premonition' (qtd. in Szondi 12), as Marcel realises that he 'does not stand outside of time, but is subject to its laws' (qtd. in Szondi 12). It seems that the 'past' does not really past; it will always be a part of Marcel.

History is like a very long river. Day after day, life repeats itself with a rhythm in the city, in the walk of a viewer. For Walter Benjamin, the city of Paris definitely demonstrates what he meant by the sense of history. Through a number of public and private events, one can see architectural developments in this capital of the nineteenth-century, such as the use of iron and the construction of the arcade. History is conceptualised by visible objects of one's everyday life, as in 'commodities' (Benjamin 152). The 'phantasmagoria' of 'commodity fetishism', as in Graeme Gilloch's reading, comes to refer Paris as a city of 'dream-architecture' (Gilloch 94), reinforcing modernity as 'a series of dream-like visions of the metropolitan environment' (Gilloch 94). Benjamin here gives us a metaphorical sense to history, revealing the sense of time in 'the ambiguity' of 'the social relationships and products' (Benjamin 157).

Salvador Dali's *The Persistence of Memory* (in Reichold and Graf 179) shows the dream image of the unconsciousness in a significant way, deconstructing the linear sense of time. In this respect, the past can be twisted and used, in order to narrate the present. In the moment of writing, the past also comes out to meet the present moment, synthesising one's own personal history as a whole. History comes from the narrator who tells the story, as in Henry James's *Autobiography*. The narrator somehow becomes a historical self, revealing the relation between personal narrative and fictional narrative. James's personal account of the past indicates a specific aesthetics of depicting memory. His story is the enormous gaze, through which the reader is able to cross the channel of history, to have a taste of his 'life lived' (Blasing xi). The sense of history comes from self-consciousness. As James's own personal literature shows, the subject and the consciousness are deeply rooted in social experiences—namely, travelling, family's past, and so on. James's early 'social consciousness' (James 9) and his mature point of view construct his 'literary portraiture' (qtd. in Dupee xi) of the self. As I look at a photograph in James's autobiography, *Henry James and His Father (From a Daguerreotype Taken in 1854)*, I start wondering if James himself, as a boy, could see his own future adventures in America and in Europe? His right hand is on his father's shoulder. Both father and son have smiles with ease and confidence, as if they are expecting something good to happen. Does James, as a small boy, know that he is about to step his little 'steps', starting from his 'New York *flâneries*'

(James 16) and more? James's 'literary portraiture', in this respect, 'leaves' the same 'room for the reader's enactment of history' (Buelens 9).

To conclude, historical narrative represents the past. In the text, different impressions of the past have been caught at different moments of the present, providing multiple perspectives, creating a coherent sense of the self. History helps the reader to see the way things were, in order to understand one's own current situation. Literature and art, as expressions of lived reality, give meaning to the essence of being.

Works Cited

Benjamin, Walter. 'A Short History of Photography'. *Screen* 13.1 (1972): 5-26.

---. 'Paris, Capital of the Nineteenth-Century'. *Reflections*. Trans. Edmund Jephcott. New York: Schocken Books, 1986.

Blasing, Mutlu Konuk. *The Art of Life: Studies in American Autobiographical Literature.* Austin & London: University of Texas Press, 1977.

Buelens, Gert. Introduction. *Enacting History in Henry James: narrative, Power, and Ethics.* Ed. Gert Buelens. Cambridge: Cambridge University Press, 1997.

Buonarroti, Michelangelo. *The Sonnets of Michelangelo.* Trans. Elizabeth Jennings. London: The Folio Society, 1961.

Da Vinci, Leonardo. *The Da Vinci Notebooks.* Ed. Emma Dickens. London: Profile Books, 2005.

Dupee, F. W. Introduction. *Autobiography*. By Henry James. Ed. F. W. Dupee. London: W. H. Allen, 1956.

Freud, Sigmund. *The Standard Edition of The Complete Psychological Works of Sigmund Freud: Five Lectures on Psycho-Analysis, Leonardo da Vinci: Volume XI (1910)*. Trans. James Strachey in collaboration with Anna Freud. London: The Hogarth Press and The Institute of Psycho-Analysis, 1957.

James, Henry. *Autobiography*. Ed. F. W. Dupee. London: W. H. Allen, 1956. Reichold, Klaus and Bernhard Graf. *Paintings that Changed the World: From Lascaux to Picasso*. Munich: Prestel, 2003.

Szondi, Peter. 'Hope in the Past: on Walter Benjamin'. Trans. Harvey Mendelsohn. *Berlin Childhood around 1900*. Cambridge, MA: Belknap of Harvard University Press, 2006.

Woolf, Virginia. *Mrs Dalloway's Party*. London: Vintage, 2010.

A Moment of Joy

· Chapter 2 ·

Jane Eyre:
Arts in the Novel of Charlotte Brontë

I want to demonstrate the way in which 'art' is seen as an expression of the inner self. The main character Jane Eyre's psychology, through Charlotte Brontë's verbal art and the narrator 'I', comes to show the complicated art of Brontë's novel. I focus on the relation between the external and the internal worlds. Through arts, the reader can see that there are at least two kinds of paintings and portraits: one aims to represent what the external world looks like, while the other serves to depict one's own thoughts and imaginations.

Critics mentioned about the role of the eye, visual objects and visual arts in Charlotte Brontë's novels. Among them, Peter J Bellis, in his article 'In the Window-Seat: Vision and Power in *Jane Eyre'*, argues that through Lacan's usage of the gaze, the reader can see the social meaning of Jane's gaze. Crucial moments of the gaze in the novel, according to Bellis, come to define the relation between the inner and the outer spheres in Brontë's writing. For example, Jane's window seat at Gateshead in the breakfast room, behind the curtain, shows a 'boundary' (Bellis 640) between her imaginary world and the external world. The curtain allows her to have 'visual access to the outside world' (Bellis 640). On the other hand, it also keeps her eye on 'the book in her lap' (Bellis 640).

For Alison Byerly, Jane's approaches to visual images show a strong sense of 'an imaginative truth', in a way in which visual arts—including illustrations in a book such as Thomas Bewick's *History of British Birds* or Jane's own landscape sketches—are 'artificial, theatrical world[s] of exterior representation from the real world of inner feeling' (Byerly 97). George Levine, in his 'Realism, or, in Praise of Lying: Some Nineteenth Century Novels', also claims that 'realism' is a 'notion of mimesis in literary art' (Levine 355). Literature, in the sense of realism as a form of verbal arts, has its feature of recording reality, as the reader can see in Henry James's novels. And yet, art can also be seen as a mimesis of nature. It is also artificial. It is a lie in Oscar Wilde's sense, since '[e]very detail is chosen and arranged by the novelist' (Levine 356), creating a reality which belongs to the novelistic world.

Charlotte Brontë's sense of reality comes from a tension between the inner desire—'inner urgencies' as in Robert B Heilman's term—and the 'observed outer life' (qtd. in Levine 361). I would suggest, Jane Eyre's inner world represents a power of her own, allowing her to overcome class differences and the boundary between imagination and reality. The master/ slave dialectic is particularly significant, when one sees Jane's paintings as representations of her non-linguistic power. When Jane is with Rochester, she cannot say things which are against Rochester. In the realm of the symbolic order, language comes to reveal class and gender differences, as Jane is the governess and Rochester is the Master. A governess is somehow treated as a high-level servant, who has 'a use value and an exchange value'

(Allen 111). Jane needs to earn money from the Master. As Jane needs to go back to Gateshead to see the Reeds, Rochester becomes her 'banker for forty pounds' (Brontë, *Jane Eyre* 223). The governess, at this moment, is an object which has exchange values. The position of Jane, in the realm of the symbolic, is the Other, the passive and the oppressed.

Jane is happy and 'self-satisfied' (Brontë, *Jane Eyre* 128) when she paints. Representing the imaginary, Jane's portfolio contains her fantasy of 'artist's dream-land' (Brontë, *Jane Eyre* 128), affecting Rochester deeply while responding her works of art in the library. Through visual arts, Jane and Rochester become spiritually united, in a way which gender and class differences are dismissed. Visual elements in Jane's paintings, such as the 'vision of the Evening Star', the 'grassy hill with a large expanse of deep blue twilit sky', and 'a bust-length view of a woman' (qtd. in Kromm 379), all come to reveal the Romantic sense of love and tranquility through nature, transcending the realistic and the mechanical external world to a 'pre-social' self, as the self is 'free also to progress, move through the class-structure' (Eagleton 39).

The relation between space and psyche is significant, in a way which Jane's inner world is accommodated through the environment, as the interior comes to serve as a private space, revealing Jane's shifting moods. For Charlotte Brontë, I would argue, the interior which the self is located in not only show as physical surroundings, but also a sense of inner reality. Visual objects characterise Jane's mood and her 'faculty of reflection' (Brontë, *Jane Eyre* 320). For instance, Jane 'pauses' her 'strange fears' 'in the centre of the obscured ceiling' (Brontë, *Jane Eyre* 316) in her room, during the night before she leaves Rochester. The ceiling is transformed from a visible object to an imaginary cinema screen, revealing Jane's imagination and her childhood memory with a cinematic technique, known as flashback—a cinematic way which Marcel Proust also uses in his auto-biographical novel, *Remembrance of Things Past*. The childhood memory of the red-room 'trauma' (Moglen 48) at Gateshead comes back to Jane, as her room in Thornfield at that moment is no longer 'a heaven' (Brontë, *Jane Eyre* 317), although it used to be. Leaving Rochester, Jane is 'weeping' in her mind (Brontë, *Jane Eyre* 318), reminding the reader her 'silent tears' (Brontë, *Jane Eyre* 22) after the nightmarish mood of 'humiliation, self-doubt, forlorn depression' (Brontë, *Jane Eyre* 18) in the red room, as the visual objects in the 'interior space' (Malane 91) re-define the room as a mental space.

When the desire of love cannot be fulfilled, Thornfield becomes a space which represents Gothic 'mental terrors' (Brontë, *Jane Eyre* 282). In Jane's dream, it somehow transforms to a place of terror, as she walks into the psychological place 'on a moonlight night, through the grass-grown enclosure within' (Brontë, *Jane Eyre* 280). The front is 'a shell-like wall, very high and very fragile-looking' (Brontë, *Jane Eyre* 280). Jane's childhood fear seems to become 'the unknown little child' she carries in her dream.

The most significant Gothic element in this novel is the 'vampire' image of the 'shape' of a woman, who is 'tall and large, with thick and dark hair hanging long down her back (Brontë, *Jane Eyre* 281). Her face, as in Jane's dream image, is 'a discoloured face', a 'savage face' with a pair of fearful 'red eyes' (Brontë, *Jane Eyre* 281). The woman's shape is 'purple', the 'lips were swelled and dark; the brow furrowed: the black eyebrows widely raised over the bloodshot eyes' (Brontë, *Jane Eyre* 281). This woman with a purple shape is the Gothic symbol of unfulfilled love and passion, reminding in me the painting of the Symbolists. Among them, Carlos Schwabe's *Study for The Wave, Feminine Figure* (Mixed media on board, 66.2 x 48 cm, Musée d'Art et d'Historie, Geneva, in Gibson 143) and Edvard Munch's *Madonna* (Colour lithograph, 60.7 x 44.5 cm, Munch-Museet, Oslo, in Gibson 145) indicate Jane's dream-like unconscious and the allegorical meaning of her vision. The vampire woman shape implies Jane's temporary lost of love, with emotional and painful reactions. The long hair and the uncanny facial expression of the woman in Schwabe's feminine figure come to show a vision of the horror, echoing the vampire woman shape which Jane sees. Munch's *Madonna* is another image, which comes to parallel Jane's vision of the vampire woman with unfulfilled sexuality. In the painting, the woman is trapped in the black background and the brown frame. The little child-like figure at the corner of the left hand side also indicates the 'unknown little child' in Jane's arm. It represents a figure which expresses fear and uncertainty.

Brontë's own painting-in-words visualizes the interaction between the inner and the outer worlds through Jane's vision. It reveals the sense of the Real, in a way which both material and emotional aspects of things are included. Brontë achieves Beauty through the narrative form of the novel, synthesising literary skills in artistic terms. The first-person narrative point of view somehow suggests that the novel can be read as Jane Eyre's autobiography, creating a vivid verbal portrait of Jane as a female teacher, who earns her own living as an independent woman. As Elizabeth Gaskell has stated in *The Life of Charlotte Brontë*, the duty of a governess is to 'realise' and to endure 'the dark side of "respectable" human nature; under no great temptation to crime, but daily giving way to selfishness and ill-temper, till its conduct towards those dependent on it sometimes amounts to a tyranny of which one would rather be the victim than the inflicter' (Gaskell 136 - 137). Both visual and verbal arts in this novel show the portrait of Jane, this governess, through the interaction between the inner and the outer worlds.

Works Cited

Allen, Dennis W. 'Jane Eyre and the Politics of Style'. *Approaches to Teaching Brontë's* Jane Eyre. Eds. Diane Long Hoeveler and Beth Lau. New York: The Modern Language Association of America, 1993.

Bellis, Peter J. 'In the Window-Seat: Vision and Power in *Jane Eyre*'. *ELH* 54.3 (1987): 639-652.

Bloom, Harold, ed. *Charlotte Brontë's* Jane Eyre. New York: Chelsea House Publishers, 1987.

Brontë, Charlotte. *Jane Eyre*. London: Penguin, 1994.

Byerly, Alison. *Realism, Representation, and the Arts in Nineteenth-Century Literature*. Cambridge: Cambridge University Press, 2006.

Eagleton, Terry. '*Jane Eyre*: A Marxist Study'. Bloom 29-45.

Gaskell, Elizabeth. *The Life of Charlotte Brontë*. Oxford: Oxford University Press, 2009.

Gibson, Michael. *Symbolism*. Köln: Taschen, 2006. Kromm, Jane. 'Visual Culture and Scopic Custom in "Jane Eyre" and "Villette"'. *Victorian Literature and Culture* 26.2 (1998): 369-394.

Levine, George. 'Realism, or, in Praise of Lying: Some Nineteenth Century Novels'. *College English* 31.4 (1970): 355-365.

Malane, Rachel. *Sex in Mind: the Gendered Brain in Nineteenth-Century Literature and Mental Sciences*. New York: Peter Lang, 2005.

Moglen, Helene. 'The End of *Jane Eyre* and the Creation of a Feminist Myth'. Bloom 47-61.

A Moment of Joy

· Chapter 3 ·

Teaching English and Cultural Exchange in Gaziantep

English teaching is a global issue. And yet, it has local concerns, in terms of cultural exchange which happens in teaching. My aim is to show the way in which cultural exchange happens in speaking. Through looking at teaching English speaking, we can understand that English teaching is not a one-way street, in which language teachers give the knowledge that they have to the students, and the main focus is to pass the exam. On the contrary, it is a win-win situation for both teachers and students, as one sees English not as a representation of dominate power. It is a tool, which one can use to create possible interactions between different cultures, as one has the motivation of teaching, learning and sharing experiences.

I. Introduction

One day I was assigned to teach an English speaking class in Gaziantep. It was a short notice. My aim was as simple as to get students to talk. In the class I met the students for the first time. I realised that we all come from very different cultural backgrounds. In the English speaking class, as students worked 'in small groups', two things are emerged, in terms of 'the experiences'—the first is about 'the experiences, both good and bad, of a person from your country living abroad'; the second is that 'a person from abroad living in your country' (O'Brien 58). Students started to think about their own past, trying to list good and bad experiences while living abroad, or seeing foreigners living in their countries. I was amazed while listening to their discussions and presentations, going from one point to another. The conversation leads them to share their own experiences. One student from Gaziantep made a point that living in Italy makes him see things differently. Another teacher from Romania in the class made a comment that Gaziantep is a city which changes rapidly. For me, these different points of view represent different cultural backgrounds, showing several stages of 'adjusting to a new culture' (O'Brien 58).

II. The Importance of Speaking

Speaking is one of the most basic ways of communication. People use languages to express their feelings, to exchange ideas and to share information. In Gaziantep, people somehow understand that my native language is not Turkish. For example, when I go to the supermarket, children see me and they say 'Hello' to me, instead of 'Merhaba'. But interestingly, there are occasions when people think I am a Turkish speaker. They ask me about 'time' ('saat') in Turkish, for example, when they see me and my husband walking in the park. I do not know if I do look like a Turkish speaker, or if they just want to talk, or if they are really desperate to know about time. At school, when students and visitors see me, they normally have two kinds of reactions when they speak. The first one is 'no English', as if they know these two words best in English. Or, some people ask me 'Türkçe biliyor musun?' ('Do you speak Turkish?'), to show that they cannot speak in English.

As a foreigner and an English teacher in Gaziantep, I fall into a pattern which many foreigners may have been through. Something as simple as 'where are you from' or 'do you speak English' may be the only few sentences that a Turkish student can say. These questions may be basic, but they are something 'personal'—for example, 'How old are you? Are you married? Do you like Turkey? Where is your family?' These so-called 'routine' questions are most of the time the 'starting point of a conversation' (Baker 107).

In Gaziantep, students are in general not confident of using English in the class, including speaking in English in the class, and listening to their teachers speaking ONLY in English in the class. In Taiwan, I used to have students who came from different countries and their native languages are not English. In the class they were very eager to learn English as a foreign language. Sometimes they even spoke to me in English, about what they have picked up from their friends—some Chinese words for instance, as a part of their language learning experience in their daily life. It seems that in general, people think that when they do not understand English, Turkish language comes to rescue. Students are highly conscious about what they see in English, since there are similar and different logics in the use of English and Turkish. They seem to learn the language in an analytical way, even through translation, as if word-for-word translation is possible. As far as I can see, Turkish is like a life buoy ('can simidi'), for students in the class who are not used to swim in the sea of English. For people just start learning how to swim, it may look normal. But we all know that if the life buoy is always available, people may not be able to learn at all.

III. Cultural Exchange in Speaking

Cultural exchange happens when I speak to students in English. They tried to listen to me carefully, in order to understand my English. Gül is my first student in Gaziantep, who is so willing to learn English with me. When we met for the first lesson, I told her that the way of learning English is to 'let yourself go'. She did not quite understand what I meant by that. Her spelling and reading are good, but she cannot freely express herself while speaking in English. She is used to think in Turkish, translating her thought into English, and put them into English words. Her way is actually making things difficult for her, especially in terms of speaking. At the first place, I encourage her to speak whatever she has in her mind, using English words that she knows. After that I tell her the correct way of saying that in English. For instance, she makes a sentence like 'I go check'. The better way of saying it can be 'I will go and check it for you'. She also says things like 'Tomato, don't like'. Actually she meant 'I don't like tomato'. She uses a phrase such as 'a yammy restaurant'. Actually she wants to say that the 'food' in the restaurant is very delicious. She loves music but she expresses her interest by saying 'listening to the computer'. I understand that she wants to say 'downloading and listening to the music from the internet'. I am sure that she recognises the correct sentence when she reads it. And yet, in Gaziantep, she will need to create a good English speaking environment of her own for practicing, in order to get a coffee from Starbucks in reality.

In the process of English teaching, cultural exchange is, in my opinion, the 'real thing' that makes teaching and learning go a long way. During our conversation I have learnt that Gül's favourite dish is 'Dolma'. Her mother prepares this lovely dish when there is an occasion to celebrate. Moreover, she introduces me her favourite book, *Da Vinci Code*. She enjoys reading that book so much, especially in Turkish translation. It has the cultural depth, expressing through symbols, images, settings and plots. We talked about the 'Epilogue' of the novel, because it is the moment of revelation of Robert Landon, the Harvard professor in the fiction. The way of representing his revelation in the novel is different from the way in which movie has shown. In the movie, Robert is shaving. When he sees his blood dropping onto the sink, he realises that what he has been looking for is 'a perfect straight line' (Brown 589) of blood, of history and of geography.

In the novel, Robert 'awoke with' 'the strangest thought' (Brown 588). The reader does not know why Robert thinks that way. One can only see phrases such as *'Could it be?'* and *'Impossible'*, implying Robert's thought. The 'sacred path' in Robert's mind is *'The earth's original prime meridian. The first zero longitude of the world. Paris's ancient Rose Line'* (Brown 589). Through this 'line', Robert realises that 'The Holy Grail 'neath ancient Roslin waits' (Brown 589). Rose is the symbol of 'the sacred feminine' (Brown 410), for women are able to 'produce life from her womb made her sacred' (Brown 411). The Rose, for the Romans, is *'la fleur des secrets'*, guarding 'privacy', as they used to hang a rose on the door when they did not want to be disturb (Brown 274). The Rose is a way to show 'respect' to each other and to 'trust' each other (Brown 274). Through his character Robert, Brown makes the link between the Rose and the Grail. In the novel, Robert explains to Sophie that

> *Rosa rugosa*, one of the oldest species of rose, had five petals and pentagonal symmetry, just like the guiding star of Venus, giving the Rose strong iconographic ties to *womanhood*. In addition, the Rose had close ties to the concept of 'true direction' and navigating one's way. The Compass Rose helped travellers navigate, as did Rose Lines, the longitudinal lines on maps. For this reason, the Rose was a symbol that that spoke of the Grail on many levels—secrecy, womanhood and guidance—the feminine chalice and guiding star that led to secret truth (Brown 274-275).

In Gaziantep, people believe that the Rose is the Prophet. It is interesting to see that the same Rose has a dual meaning, representing both male and female in different cultures and religious believes. And yet, the Prophet (known as 'Güllerin Efendisi', 'Master of Roses') is the person who delivers the words of God. There is a famous portrait about the Ottoman Empire Sultan, Fatih Sultan Mehmed, by the chief painter 'Sinan Bey' in the 15th century (see this portrait in İrepoğlu 52). Sultan Mehmet 'the Conqueror' smells the Rose in the picture, as embracing the spiritual joy that the Prophet tries to show people. The dual meaning of the Rose, I would argue in both cultures, is that the symbol 'covers' what it supposes to 'show' (or to 'say')—the divine revelation of seeing 'God as creator' (Tillich 73). The Rose also symbolises a woman's womb, having the power of creation which remains the secret of God. And yet, when we look at the land itself, not civilizations such as 'Byzantine churches' to 'Ottoman palaces', we realise that the ancient Anatolia celebrates 'Mother Goddess culture' 'nearly ten thousand years ago' (Voss 132) through 'hamam', known as 'the Turkish bath'. The image of the bathing women shows 'the divine feminine' (Voss 132), reminding in me the French painter

Paul Cézanne and his *Bathers* (1894-1905, in Robbins, Cat. 43). Cézanne has painted the earth in brown, making the colour similar to the huge, statue-like, rock-shaped female figures of his bathers. In the painting the 'woman's brown face and arm evoke the brownness of the land' (Lin 34). The inner divinity and beauty of 'womanliness' are conveyed through landscape, showing the male painter's love to his mother earth. Gül and I come to understand ourselves better, when we see this symbolic meaning of Rose in both cultures.

Gül also shows me a photo of her dear friend, which was taken by a classmate, emerging wonderful memories of her high school years. Through talking about things which are related to her life and her culture, she can express herself in a better way. In this case, English is not only a difficult symbol for her, which is used by people from a different world. She can make sense of it by making it meaningful. It contains her own experience and her own story. Cultural exchange, in my view, is to recognise similar spirits through different social activities. For example, I recognise pine trees in Gaziantep as 'Christmas trees', because of my educational and cultural backgrounds. During 'Ramazan' period, in the evening family and friends get together to have 'Iftar' meal. The poor can also receive free 'Iftar', as people and the government make their donations. After thirty days of 'Ramazan', people in Gaziantep eat 'yuvarlama' and 'pilav' for breakfast on the first day of Bayram. Moreover, during 'Kurban Bayram', known as 'sacrifice festival', people give meat to the poor. Bayram, like Christmas, is a religious holiday, which represents God's love and mercy. As in Fatih Akın's film *The Edge of Haven*, one can see that the German mother asks the Turkish-German literature professor, why people go to the mosque and prey, particularly on Friday? As God shows his mercy to İbrahim, the prophet does not have to sacrifice his son. Instead, God has sent the sheep to rescue and to be sacrificed. Nowadays during Christmas holiday people decorate Christmas trees, exchange gifts, see family and friends; as during Bayram holiday people are with their family and friends, having chocolate and sweets to enjoy and to celebrate life.

I encourage students, especially University students, to

have their own way of seeing and thinking. For instance, in the class, students read an article, 'Who Knows You Better, Your Family or Your Friends'? Students can understand the main idea of the article—such as 'Who can choose the right girl for Richard' (Oxenden, Latham-Koenig and Seligson 6)? After that we have in-class discussion. Students can talk about their own experiences, come to make a point about who knows them better. For example, Fatih in the class thinks that his 'friends' know him better, because he likes the girl they introduced him. And yet, his 'family' have different considerations. The family may try to find a girl who can 'fit in', but friends may think about the type of girls that Fatih really likes. Moreover, I also encourage students to think about the issue in a different way, such as 'Do I know my family better or my friend better'? There is no so-called 'correct' answer to this question. The point is to make sure that students are able to 'think' while 'speaking', sharing their thoughts during the conversation. They may not be able to speak fluently, but the 'act' of speaking will do them good. They will need to allow themselves to think in English.

Before one can think in English, one must have enough English words in mind, in order to make sentences. And yet, English words are not just words. They are symbols which contain meanings. Meanings can be as simple as a tree, a garden, and a house. They can also be as complicated as the whole culture of dwelling. The other day I saw a student in the university cafe. He was watching a DVD. I passed by him, had an idea that he was watching an episode of an American TV series. There were two women talking. He asked me if I was able to understand what they were talking about. I said 'of course' without any thinking. He replied to me in Turkish 'but the conversation was so fast'. I did not realise it was 'so fast'. At least for me it is not. Not until he said so. On the way back to the office, his words were still in my mind. Was the speed the problem? In the conversation, one man was talking to a woman about a situation in life, which is something like 'Woolf's *Mrs Dalloway*'. I wonder if my student would understand that conversation, even if it was very slow. If he did not hear about the name 'Virginia Woolf', did not know about her as a British female writer, or about her novel, would he be able to understand the 'Englishness' of that situation (as how memories come back to the present at a certain moment of time) in the conversation, when the woman character walks on the street, talking to people and thinking about her past?

IV. Conclusion: The Meaning of Cultural Exchange

The same thing can happen when Turkish culture means something to someone. For someone who comes from an English speaking world, Turkish culture is something 'foreign' and 'exotic' (Tallack 42), as one can see in 1904, Lillian Russell's 'Turkish den', 'at her West 57th Street home' (Tallack 44). I argue, Russell's 'Turkish den' represents an imaginary world, which does not exist in her New York everyday life. Her imagination and desire of getting in touch with the other culture, through interior design, indicates the cultural discontent of her own. That corner of her house, for me, shows exactly the meaning of cultural exchange—it is the freedom of life-long exploring, learning, adventure and development. English language opens the gate for learners, to express their own experiences and cultures, making them possible for people from different cultural backgrounds to understand. The 'Turkish den' of Russell's is her inwardness—the freedom to show her emotion in a private space, from the verbal level to the visual level. Words and languages certainly communicate people. And yet, the image of the 'Turkish den' emerges meanings which beyond law and order, visualising sensations out of shared rationality.

Eastern and Western cultures are not the same, but related. My interest for Virginia Woolf and her writing took me to Turkey. As the members of the Bloomsbury Group built their 'little Cambridge' in 46 Gordon Square, Bloomsbury, London, in the summer of 1905, I tend to realise and to appreciate the culture of having a conversation. 'Talk', as Woolf addresses as those 'pipe-smoking' 'Thursday evening parties' (Lin 27), has formed a particular intellectual culture for Woolf's London society, in which 'Byzantine' is included. Here I conclude, discussions of philosophy, politics, arts and literature help one to use English in different cultures, communicating ideas and beliefs among people, no matter 'how difficult—how impossible' (Woolf 165).

Acknowledgements

I would like to thank Mr Mehmet Eren Gülşan, Mr Faruk Sadıç and Dr Ali Tolga Bozdana, for showing me the correct Turkish sentences which are written in this article.

Works Cited

Ashman, Anastasia M. and Jennifer Eaton Gökmen, eds. *Tales from the Expat Harem: Foreign Women in Modern Turkey.* Istanbul: Doğan Kitap, 2007.

Baker, Natalie. 'Sailing in Byzantium'. Ashman and Gökmen 100-110.

Brown, Dan. *The Da Vinci Code.* 2003. London: Corgi, 2004.

Easthope, Antony. *Englishness and National Culture.* London: Routledge, 1999.

Ercelebi, Ergun and Savas Uckun, eds. *Culture of Cuisine and Food of Gaziantep and Aleppo: Similarities and Differences.* Istanbul: Düzey Matbaacılık and Gaziantep University, 2008.

İrepoğlu, Gül. *Levnî: Painting Poetry Colour.* Istanbul: The Society of Friends of Topkapı Palace Museum, 1999.

Lin, Allison Tzu Yu. *Virginia Woolf and the European Avant-Garde: London, Painting, Film and Photography*. Taipei: Showwe, 2009.

Oxenden, Clive, Christina Latham-Koenig and Paul Seligson. *New English File: Pre-intermediate Student's Book*. 2005. Oxford: Oxford University Press, 2009.

O'Brien Josephine. *English for Business*. Boston: Thomson Heinle, 2007.

Pamuk, Orhan. *The Museum of Innocence*. Trans. Maureen Freely. London: Faber and Faber, 2009.

Robbins, Anne. *Cézanne in Britain*. London: National Gallery, 2006.

Tillich, Paul. *Biblical Religion and the Search for Ultimate Reality*. 1955. London: The University of Chicago Press, 1965.

Tallack, Douglas. *New York Sights: Visualizing Old and New New York*. Oxford: Berg, 2005.

Voss, Karen-Claire. 'The Goddess Metamorphosis.' Ashman and Gökmen 131-136.

Woolf, Virginia. 'Old Bloomsbury'. *Moments of Being*. Ed. Jeanne Schulkind. Sussex: Sussex University Press, 1976.

· Chapter 4 ·

Roger Fry, Istanbul, and the Art of Seeing

Biologically speaking, art is a blasphemy. We were given our eyes to see things, not to look at them.

Roger Fry, *Vision and Design*

The experience which I am attempting to describe by one tentative approach after another is very precise and is immediately recognizable. But it exists at a level of perception and feeling which is probably preverbal—hence, very much, the difficulty of writing about it.

John Berger, *About Looking*

Virginia Woolf's *Roger Fry: A Biography* depicts the transformation of her friend Roger Fry's aesthetic theory and his own paintings through his discovery of French Post-Impressionist paintings. And yet, According to Woolf, it is the trip to Constantinople, the capital of Byzantine Empire, now Istanbul, which changes Fry's mood and his way of painting after the harsh criticism he received in England. Fry was the organizer of two Post-Impressionist exhibitions. The first one opened on Tuesday 8 November 1910 in the Grafton Galleries in London. The second one opened in the same galleries on 5 October 1912. They received negative criticisms by the viewers, art critics and the general public. This paper aims to show the way in which Roger Fry's trip to Turkey turns his reputation, from a bad art critic to a 'taste maker' (Teukolsky 193). In Woolf's writing, the reader can see this point in depth. The psychological function of the trip to Turkey is to help Fry to recover from the harsh criticism, making him find his way of expressing his own emotion. After the trip, Fry's paintings construct a new style, in a way which Turkish scenes, people and things are coming into a flux of sensation of Fry's own.

In Virginia Woolf's *Roger Fry*, the reader can see a vivid

visual impression of her close friend Roger Fry in words, which was written after his death in September 1934. In Woolf's writing, it seems that she becomes 'a stranger', seeing Fry 'for the first time', in the year of 1910 (Woolf 149). Again, in her essay 'Mr Bennett and Mrs Brown' (1924), Woolf depicts a sense of 'change having taken place in human character', 'in or about December 1910' (qtd. Bullen 1). Although the meeting of Woolf and Fry may not be in December, the 'change' of 'human character' indicates two things—firstly, the person that Woolf knows, and secondly, the impact of the first Post-Impressionist exhibition, *Manet and the Post-Impressionists*, which was opened on Tuesday 8 November 1910 in the Grafton Galleries in London.

Roger Fry was 'only' forty-four years old, in the year of 1910. According to Woolf, Fry's reputation does not fit the way he looks. He is 'a man with a great weight of experience behind him' (Woolf 149). His look is a kind of confusion, because people expect him to look like someone 'who lectured upon the Old Masters at Leighton House'. In other words, Fry should be 'pale, academic, aesthetic-looking' (Woolf 149). And yet, Fry's impression happens to be totally the opposite—he looks 'brown and animated' (Woolf 149). Criticism is always hard to take, no matter in which year of one's own life. However, for someone like Roger Fry, who was quite successful in his career in England at that time, still, it was very difficult to introduce something new to the British public.

In Frances Spalding's book, *Duncan Grant: A Biography*, the reader can see that the term 'Post-Impressionism' was invented by a journalist, Robert Dell, while he was working with Fry to put on the official title of the First Post-Impressionist Exhibition, held in the Grafton Galleries off Bond Street in London. *Manet and the Post-Impressionists* was opened on Tuesday 8 November 1910, running until 15 January of the following year (MacCarthy 71). The press day was Saturday 5 November. Eight of the eleven daily newspapers reviewed the exhibition on either the 7th or the 8th, so that a substantial amount of press reaction was available to viewers before they saw the show by themselves.

According to Frances Spalding, to those who love Edwardian 'tonal gradations, elegance, naturalism, sentimental anecdotalism and mimetic veracity, Post-Impressionism seemed crude, unskilled and unreal' (Spalding 100). Spalding also accounts for the anxious reaction of the British viewing public in 1910, by suggesting that the Post-Impressionist exhibition was interpreted as a symptom of 'social and political unrest' (Spalding 100). As Spalding points out,

Britain might be enjoying a period of 'splendid isolation', but threats and anxieties were accumulating that made for an underlying nervousness. Industrial unrest had erupted in the Welsh coal-miners' strike, which was broken up that month by troops. The Irish were demanding Home Rule and the Suffragettes were gaining in strength. Only a few days after the show opened at the Grafton Galleries, the Suffragettes marched on the House of Commons while Asquith spoke on the question of Women's Rights: 117 arrests were made, the six-hour protest marking a 'Black Friday' that set off a programme of window-smashing, arson and bombs as the Suffragettes, denied political power through the normal democratic procedures, resorted to violence (Spalding 100).

The public's mind associates Post-Impressionist paintings with Socialism and Women's Suffrage. These social movements shared a common enthusiasm for changing an old order to a new one. In addition to the mental shocks the pictures brought to the British public, the Post-Impressionist pictures, particularly the works of Gauguin, Cézanne, Matisse and Picasso, drew Fry's attentions to a new aesthetic experience by their use of colour, primitive style and spatial arrangement of the canvas.

Post-Impressionist paintings represent a fresh emphasis on style, on line, on colour, on scale, on interval and on proportion, which for them has the impact of Byzantine art. As Fry commented on Cézanne and Gauguin in 'The Last Phase of Impressionism' (1908), the art works of the Post-Impressionists seem to be representing a primary form of Byzantine art. The Post-Impressionists

> are proto-Byzantines rather than Neo-Impressionists. They have already attained to the contour with willfully simplified and unmodulated masses, and reply for their whole effect upon a well-considered coordination of the simplest elements. [...]. The relations of every tone and colour are deliberately chosen and stated in unmistakable terms (Fry 375).

The Post-Impressionists use simple colours and shapes to express emotions. The difference between Impressionism lies in their way of dealing with light and shadow. C. J. Holmes in his 'Notes on the Post-Impressionist Painters: Grafton Galleries, 1910-11', also points out that

> For the moment it is enough to recognise that in the first Post-Impressionist painters we have a reaction from the

materialism which limited the original Impressionists to the rendering of natural effects of light and colour with the greatest attainable scientific truth. Within those iron limits art was bound to come to a standstill, and in setting up sincerity to personal vision as a guiding rule, in the place of sincerity to natural appearances, the Post-Impressionists were really only reverting to the principle which has inspired all the greatest art in the world (Holmes 10).

From the above quotation, the reader can see that The Impressionists paint what they see. On the other hand, the Post-Impressionists paint what they feel. Again, according to Fry, in his 'The Post-Impressionists' exhibition catalogue, he points out that the Impressionists

were interested in analysing the play of light and shadow into a multiplicity of distinct colours; they refined upon what was already illusive in nature. [...]. The Post-Impressionists on the other hand were not concerned with recording impressions of colour or light. They were interested in the discoveries helped them to express emotions which the object themselves evoked; their attitude towards nature was far more independent, not to say rebellious (Fry, 'The Post-Impressionists', 8-9).

The reader can see the difference between these two types of artists—the Impressionists capture the play of light and shadow in nature; the Post-Impressionists personalize nature with emotion. Both Fry's and Holmes's comments indicate what they saw as the fundamental difference between Impressionism and Post-Impressionism. In a speech delivered in French in Brussels during the autumn of 1933, Fry maintained that Post-Impressionists form a synthesis of the dual nature of painting, which contains not only the representation of the external visual world, but also the expression of inner emotion in an aesthetic way, revealing 'psychological situations' of the artist (Fry, 'The Double Nature of Painting', 367). Moments of vision are key moments of expressing these emotions which are contained in the simplest forms, such as—'a red poppy, a mother's reproof, a Quaker upbringing, sorrows, loves, humiliations' (Woolf 161).

The viewing public of 1910 in England definitely had a very different way of seeing works of art. They may care about arts as much as Fry did. And yet, in the year of 1910, within that particular social context of England, the public simply could not appreciate what Fry saw in Post-Impressionist paintings. By having the First Post-Impressionist exhibition, Fry shared his 'sense of revelation' (Woolf 152) with the crowd. However, in the eyes of the public, those 'bold' and 'bright' pictures shown at the Grafton Gallery are 'in contrast with the Watts portrait of a beautiful Victorian lady' (Woolf 152). For instance, the portrait *Frances, Marchioness of Bath* (1861-5, in Bryant 123) by G. F. Watts, shows the elegant quality of the lady Frances, with her 'ornate gown of the palest grey silk', revealing 'a timeless image of elegance in the spirit of eighteenth-century portraiture' (Bryant 122). The realistic representation of the lady's pearl necklace, and the wrinkles of her silk dress, certainly leads the painterly fashion of Watts' time. For the viewing public of 1910, it was almost impossible 'to make the transition from Watts to Picasso' (Woolf 152), because their styles of paintings are very different from each other. Many complaints went to the director of the galleries. Fry was taken as 'a fool' (Woolf 154), because the primitive style of the Post-Impressionists was thought as 'outrages, anarchistic and childish' (Woolf 154).

The gap between Fry's enthusiasm and the crowd's feeling of having been cheated, surely alarmed Fry himself. Fry just could not understand why the public insisted to see some 'photographic representation' of paintings, as the Victorian Masters did. For Fry, it is a real 'childish' attitude (Woolf 164). Although a real piece of art work would not concern 'narrow-minded' (Woolf 166) people, and yet, Fry's preference to the Post-Impressionists makes it difficult 'for the older artists to work with him' (Woolf 166), especially when the viewing public think that the exhibition is 'an insult' (Woolf 154). Two groups of people have very different ways of seeing a work of art, particularly showing that their definitions of 'childishness' are totally different.

Roger Fry's way of seeing and painting come closer to the Post-Impressionists, as 'the Georgians' do in literature, 'when they wish to reduce the innumerable details of a crowded landscape to simplicity—step back, half shut the eyes, gesticulate a little vaguely with the fingers, and reduce Edwardian fiction to a view' (Woolf, 'Mr Bennett and Mrs Brown' 385). The literary voyage from Edwardian realistic representation to Georgian psychological expression, has a parallel development with the transformation, from traditional Victorian academic painting to a freedom of modernist expression of emotion. As Fry's own painting *Chair with Bowl and Towel* (1916-8, in Shone 259) shows, the wrinkles of the woman sitter's dress were simplified by a few lines, paralleling the circle lines of the bowl, the towel, and the smooth back of the chair. The woman's head is resting on her right arm, showing her ease. It is a very different pose, comparing to Watts' Frances in the painting, in a way which Frances stands by a huge red chair, resting her right arm on the back of the chair, in order to look elegant and perfect. Her facial expression is a bit intense, looking tired, most probably because of standing for a long time, posing for Watts.

Fry himself definitely does not like to be called a 'pasticheur' (Woolf 175). After the storm of criticism stirred up by the first Post-Impressionist exhibition in London, Fry's trip to Constantinople—Capital of the Byzantine Empire, now Istanbul, confirmed his knowledge of Byzantine art, and his way of seeing emotion in the Post-Impressionist paintings, preparing his mood for organising the Second Post-Impressionist exhibition. In Fry's letter to Sir William Rothenstein, dated on 13 April, 1911 and written in Hotel Bristol, Constantinople, he kindly asked Sir Rothenstein to support the Second Post-Impressionist show. Although the First Exhibition did not go very well, Fry did not lose his motivation. This time, Fry was hoping to add up some young English artists' works, for helping them to be a part of 'the New English Art Club', including Walter Sickert's paintings. Fry was proposing that the exhibition will be 'divided 2 rooms to this English group and 2 rooms to the works of the younger Russian artists' (Woolf 167). Fry's point is to promote contemporary art in England. Still, the Grafton Galleries in London were chosen to host the show. But this time, Fry had 'the actual control and responsibility on behalf of the Grafton Galleries' (Woolf 167). Fry certainly lived the spirit of Constantinople in Istanbul, for the city 'was more open to talent; newcomers who proved successful were rapidly promoted' (Herrin 8), as Fry's enthusiasm implies.

Fry sympathises young artists. The Second Post-Impressionist exhibition will give them a chance to live and to paint. With his close friends, Clive Bell and Vanessa Bell, in Istanbul, Fry had a chance to learn more about Byzantine art—which serves as an answer for 'the aesthetic problems' (Woolf 169) he came across during the First Post-Impressionist exhibition. Apart from being ill, Fry was mostly satisfied with what he saw in Turkey, since the landscape and the Turkish hills 'were not romantic'. He saw 'the real light' of the sun, and 'the structure of the hills' (Woolf 171). Handcrafts are also amazing. In both French and Turkish, Fry 'persuaded the driver to take him to the native quarter', hoping to buy pots and handkerchiefs. He immediately became 'the centre of a group of excited peasants' (Woolf 171). The coloured bold pattern of the handcrafts reminds in him 'some half-forgotten tradition—Russian, or Greek, or Chinese? Whatever it was it proved that the tradition was alive and that the peasants of Broussa put the educated English to shame' (Woolf 171). I am sure Woolf meant the peasants in 'Bursa'.

Fry sees the emotion of the peasants of Turkey, as 'at the sight of a wolf without using a single adjective' as in literature—'now in Frances Cornford, now in Wordsworth, now in *Marie Clare*, a novel by Marguerite Audous' (Woolf 172). According to Woolf, it seems that Fry found a lot of 'impure associations' in words, when it comes to expressing emotion. As Clive Bell points out, painting is a 'significant form' (Bell 11), since pure colours and lines can express this emotional 'reality' fully. Fry did not really have time 'to work out his theory of the influence of Post-Impressionism upon literature' (Woolf 172). And yet, Virginia Woolf sees the new force of literature, under the influence of Post-Impressionism, in a way which the 'old clothes' of 'representation' will be gone. Both art forms—literature and painting, 'should work out the new theories side by side' (Woolf 172), in order to express 'reality' on a level of what one feels.

Leonard Woolf, Virginia Woolf's husband, was the secretary of the Second Post-Impressionist exhibition. It opened in the Grafton Galleries on 5 October 1912 in London, and ran until the end of January 1913. The show was visited by twice as many people as the first show. And yet, the reaction of the public was as negative as the 1910 exhibition. As Leonard Woolf recorded,

> Large numbers of people came to the exhibition, [...].
> Anything new in the arts, particularly if it is good,
> infuriates them and they condemn it as either immoral
> or ridiculous or both. As secretary I sat at my table in
> the large second room of the galleries prepared to deal
> with enquiries from possible purchasers or answer
> any questions about the pictures. [...]. Hardly any of
> them made the slightest attempt to look at, let alone
> understand, the pictures, and the same inane questions

or remarks were repeated to me all day long (Leonard Woolf 94).

The viewing public had very little understanding of what the Post-Impressionists were trying to show. Leonard Woolf's comments reveal moral shock of the crowd, and their negative attitude toward the controversial exhibition, particularly the themes (female nudity) and the technique (a 'primitive' way of constructing lines and shapes) of the Post-Impressionist pictures. As Jacqueline V. Falkenheim points out, the Post-Impressionist style is the 'absence of conventional modeling, and especially the intense colors and conspicuous outlines found in many of these works, were disagreeably unfamiliar to the viewing public' (Falkenheim 14). Frances Spalding also describes the outrage of the viewing public, as 'London was shocked to discover that one of its most distinguished critics had created a show', 'to destroy the whole fabric of European painting' (Spalding 1996, 37).

Real works of art aim to express human feelings and conditions, rather than to copy what things look like. Roger Fry sees the 'primitive' quality of the Post-Impressionist paintings. And yet, the quality of Byzantine art cannot be called 'primitive' at all. It is not 'primitive' enough, as in the sense of African or ancient American arts. The paradoxical element of seeing is that the city of Constantine represents the foundation of Western civilization. However, the Post-Impressionist primitive style refers to a sense of pre-historical time, touching the mood of humanity in a much more general scale. Here, humanity is probably what Fry meant by 'a universal quality in art' (Teukolsky 211). This phrase over and over again appears in Fry's essays and art writings. It certainly does not refer to a system of aesthetics, which can rule an empire of arts. Different historical period of time has its own art of seeing. For instance, the taste changed from one era to another, from the eighteen-century 'historical grand style' (Sambrook 147) to Edwardian realism; from Victorian aesthetics to Georgian modernism, as Virginia Woolf's 'Mr Bennett and Mrs Brown' implies. In literature, writers and critics are also searching for a new way of seeing—a method of constructing a new taste which suits their own creativity.

Certainly, Fry came to Constantinople 'to see things, not to look at them' (Fry, 'The Artist's Vision' 32). Richard Shone also points out that

> Fry's May 1911 visit to Turkey, where he saw Byzantine mosaics and was excited by the landscape around Brusa, made an immediate impact on his painting. After his return, several large canvases were carried out from sketches made in Turkey which emphasise linear structure and schematic form at the expense of representational detail and local colour (Shone 57).

In Shone's book, 'Bursa' is spelled wrongly, and I cannot find any examples of Fry's 'sketches made in Turkey which emphasise linear structure and schematic form at the expense of representational detail and local colour' in the same book. And yet, it does not really matter if Fry painted Turkish landscapes or not. The point is, what did he see in Turkish pots and handkerchiefs? Is it something that exist within the general humanity—the 'Beauty' (Lin 42) which touched his own 'petit sensation' (Woolf 174)—that 'some half-forgotten tradition' (Woolf 171). Virginia Woolf cannot define this 'tradition'. I think it is still within the general scale of humanity—in simplicity and in sincere expression of emotion in arts. Beauty, as Woolf claims in her essay 'The Cinema', is that sort of 'queer sensation' which will 'continue to be beautiful whether we behold it or not' (Woolf, 'The Cinema' 349). Art certainly cannot do without life. Fry's historical imaginations of ancient civilization, such as Byzantine art, come to justify the historical images of primitivism. With his life-long experiences of being a professional artist and art critic, what Fry experienced after the Post-Impressionist exhibitions pushed him to see what was left out, as 'a free man thinks of death least of all things; and his wisdom is a meditation not of death but life' (Woolf 298).

Works Cited

Bell, Clive. *Art*. London: Chatto & Windus, 1947. Bryant, Barbara. *G. F. Watts Portraits: Fame & Beauty in Victorian Society*. London: National Portrait Gallery, 2004.

Bullen, J. B., ed. *Post-Impressionists in England: The Critical Reception*. London: Routledge, 1988.

Falkenheim, Jacqueline V. *Roger Fry and the Beginnings of Formalist Art Criticism*. Ann Arbor: UMI, 1980.

Fry, Roger. 'The Last Phase of Impressionism' (1908). *The Burlington Magazine*. March 1908, 374-375.

---. 'The Post-Impressionists'. *Exhibition Catalogue: Manet & the Post-Impressionists, London, 1910-11*, 7-13. Hyman Kreitman Research Centre for the Tate Library and Archive, Tate Britain, London.

---. 'The Double Nature of Painting'. *Apollo* May 1969, 362-371.

---. *Vision and Design*. Ed. J. B. Bullen. New York: Dover, 1981.

Herrin, Judith. *Byzantium: The Surprising Life of a Medieval Empire*. London: Penguin, 2008.

Holmes, C. J. 'Notes on the Post-Impressionist Painters: Grafton Galleries, 1910-11'. *For the Exhibition, Manet & the Post-Impressionists, London, 1910-11*, 7-17. Hyman Kreitman Research Centre for the Tate Library and Archive, Tate Britain, London.

Lin, Allison Tzu Yu. *Virginia Woolf and the European Avant-Garde: London, Painting, Film and Photography*. Taipei: Showwe, 2009.

MacCarthy, Desmond. 'The Post-Impressionist Exhibition of 1910'. *The Bloomsbury Group: A Collection of Memoirs, Commentary and Criticism*. Ed. S. P. Rosenbaum. London: University of Toronto Press (Croom Helm Ltd.), 1975.

Sambrook, James. *The Eighteenth Century: the Intellectual and Cultural Context of English Literature, 1700- 1789*. London: Longman, 1986.

Shone, Richard. *The Art of Bloomsbury: Roger Fry, Vanessa Bell and Duncan Grant*. London: Tate Gallery, 1999.

Spalding, Frances. *British Art Since 1900*. London: Thames and Hudson, 1996.

---. *Duncan Grant: A Biography*. London: Pimlico, 1998.

Teukolsky, Rachel. *The Literate Eye: Victorian Art Writing and Modernist Aesthetics*. Oxford: Oxford University Press, 2009.

Woolf, Leonard. *Beginning Again: An Autobiography of the Years 1911-1918*. London: Hogarth Press, 1964.

Woolf, Virginia. 'Mr Bennett and Mrs Brown' (1924). *The Essays of Virginia Woolf, Vol III*. Ed. Andrew McNeillie. London: The Hogarth Press, 1986-1994, 4 volumes.

---. 'The Cinema' (1926). *The Essays of Virginia Woolf, Vol IV*. Ed. Andrew McNeillie. London: The Hogarth Press, 1986-1994, 4 volumes.

---. *Roger Fry* (1940). London: Vintage, 2003.

A Moment of Joy

· Chapter 5 ·

The Dialectical Relation: Landscape and History in *The Last of the Mohicans* and *The Course of Empire*

The Present, which, as a model of Messianic time, comprises the entire history of mankind in an enormous abridgement, coincides exactly with the stature which the history of mankind has in the universe.

-Walter Benjamin

I read James Fenimore Cooper's novel *The Last of the Mohicans* and Thomas Cole's series of paintings, *The Course of Empire*, from the perspective of the dialectical relation between landscape and history. Landscape is a truly unique feature of

America. Through Cooper's and Coles' works, the reader can see a vision of historical progress, which requires a landscape standpoint. In other words, history comes into landscape through artistic representations. Landscape is an intersection of history and the artists. Through the standpoint of landscape, the novelist and the painter cast their eyes on history. At the same time, history also fixes its eyes on them. Holding American landscape in mind, Cooper and Cole are also making themselves as great artists in the history of American literature and painting.

I. Thesis: J. F. Cooper's Picturesque Landscape

Now I am ready for composing this paper—in which I want to deal with the relationship between landscape and history in Cooper's *The Last of the Mohicans*. The first idea I want to address is the concept of history. At this moment, this novel does not only lie on my desk, it also has a position within the greatest world literature. History is, as John Mc Williams argues, 'in the largest sense, the study of the consequences of the passage of time' (Williams 98).

As I sit here and write this paper, what I can see is not only my present 'time', but also Cooper's 'time' and the 'time' of the historical event in this novel—1757 Massacre. According to Heidegger, this moment, the present, is not a measureable unit, but a situation of 'being'. History, in *The Last of the Mohicans*, can be seen as a construction of human actions and movements. The most obvious historical event, in Cooper's novel, should be the Massacre in 1757. In Cooper's novel, history means battles and combats between different groups of human beings, with different skin colors—say, red verses white; between different empires—they are British and French; between different political alliances—which are empires with different Indian tribes; and the last but not the least, among the Indians.

Cooper's portrayal of American landscape has a significant quality of dualism. On one hand, it has been portrayed in a pure picturesque mode, which indicates landscape in its pure form, as if it is standing outside of a sense of history. And yet, on the other hand, landscape itself is not only an association and an agent of history or fiction, but also a standpoint for Cooper to approach history. In other words, Cooper made his landscape a subject, which is not only a setting where things like Duncan's dream of 'a knight of ancient chivalry, holding his midnight vigils before the tent of a re-captured princess' (Cooper, *Mohicans* 147) would happen. The question I want to ask is that, did Cooper indicate a vision of history through his portrayal of landscape? What kind of sense of history did he bring to his readers?

There are many picturesque sites in *The Last of the Mohicans* which Cooper designed for the 'sequent episodes of his narrative—and that in any case, have been eclipsed in most readers' minds by the splendor of Gleen's Falls' (Nevius 9). In Wayne Franklin's observation, there is a very interesting anecdote, which is related to the background of Cooper's using Lake George and Gleen's Falls in the novel. 'He first visited Lake George,' as Franklin claims, 'and other parts of his setting in the upper Hudson valley in 1824 with four touring Britons, and it was during this tour—indeed, just as Cooper and one of the Englishmen stood "in the caverns at Gleens falls"—that Cooper had determined to write the book' (Franklin 29).

Actually, through Cooper's picturesque mode of portraying the landscape, the reader can see that the landscape per se seems to have nothing to do with history, because he described landscape from a perspective of a tourist. When Hawk-eye's party came to the Gleen's Dalls for escaping from the Indians, the way that Hawk-eye described the Falls was a sort of tourist appreciation:

> You can easily see the cunning of the place—the rock is black lime-stone, which every body knows is soft, it makes no uncomfortable pillow, where brush and pine wood is scarce; well, the fall was once a few yards below us, and I dare to say was, in its time, as regular and as handsome a sheet of water as any along the Hudson (Cooper, Mohicans, 64).

Here is Hawk-eye's further description of the remarkable water—

Ay! there are the falls on two sides of us, and the river above and below. If you had daylight, it would be worth the trouble to step up on the height of this rock, and look at the perversity of the water! It falls by no rule at all; sometimes it leaps, sometimes it tumbles; there, it skips; here, it shoots; in one place 'tis white as snow, and in another 'its green as grass; …. Ay, lady, the fine cobweb-looking cloth you wear at your throat, is coarse, and like a fish net, to little spots I can show you, where the river fabricates all sorts of images, as if, having broke loose from order, it would try its hand at everything (Cooper, Mohicans 64).

Hawk-eye's description of 'this picturesque and remarkable little cataract (Cooper, Mohicans 65) does not have any relation with history, which is his party's escaping from the Indians. The relation between the picturesque landscape and history is uncoordinated. The reaction of Hawk-eye's auditors was even bizarre while they 'received a cheering assurance of the security of their place of concealment from his untutored description of Glenn's, they were much inclined to judge differently from Hawk-eye, of its wild beauties' (Cooper, Mohicans 65). The 'wild beauties' of the landscape have nothing to do with the security of Hawk-eye's party. Here the picturesque vision that Cooper brought to the reader has nothing to do with history and with human action.

The uncoordinated relation between landscape and history comes from Cooper's way of portrayal the landscape, as he made it with a point of view of a traveler. Here is another example:

The tourist, the valetudinarian, or the amateur of the beauties of nature, who, in the train of his four-in-hand, now rolls through the scenes we have attempted to describe, in quest of information, health, or pleasure, or floats steadily towards his object on those artificial waters, which have sprung up under the administration of a statesman, who has dared to stake his political character on the hazardous issue, is not to suppose that his ancestors traversed those hills, or struggled with the same currents with equal facility (Cooper, Mohicans 167).

The tourist can see the beauty of the wild landscape, to appreciate the power of nature without thinking about how to conquer the land or to fight against the enemy. Another scene also indicates the uncoordinated relation between landscape and history is the scene of British and French armies' trace. As Cooper depicted, 'the scene was at once animated and still. All that pertained to nature was sweet or simply grand, while those parts which depended on the temper and movements of man, were lively and playful' (Cooper, Mohicans 168). Here the reader can see that landscape is 'animated and still', which has nothing to do with 'movements of man'.

The wilderness in *The Last of Mohicans* has been portrayed as a subject, not a setting for a narrative scene. When people approach the wilderness, the wilderness seems to approach them at the same time. For instance, when the British army entered into the woods, they marched 'until the notes of their fifes growing fainter in distance, the forest at length appeared to swallow up the living mass which had slowly entered its bosom'. Besides, the wilderness is an agent, an 'intermediate space' (Cooper, Mohicans 33) between history and fiction. In the beginning of the novel, Cooper reminded the reader that

> It was a feature peculiar to the colonial wars of North America, that the toils and dangers of the wilderness were to be encountered, before the adverse hosts could meet. A wild, and, apparently, an impervious boundary of forests, severed the possessions of the hostile provinces of France and England (Cooper, *Mohicans* 15).

Cooper portrayed the wilderness to connect historical events with his fictional plots and characters. The result is as the subtitle of his novel, 'A Narrative of 1757'. Although the wilderness can be seen as an agency, an association, and the 'intermediate space' between history and Cooper's fiction, the wilderness itself 'stands outside' (Martin 50) the progress of human history. The wilderness is the standstill, which does not involve in history.

II. Thomas Cole's Historical Landscape

The relation between landscape and history is very different in the cases of European and American culture. History was 'considered the essence of European culture, and most picturesque European landscapes contained crumbling ruins and ancient landmarks alluding to the past' (Asleson and Moore 15). Thomas Cole, an intelligent landscape painter in Cooper's period, painted *The Course of Empire*, which has been considered by Cooper as 'the highest genius this country has ever produced', 'one of the noblest works of art that has ever been wrought' (Beard 398). Works like this series of paintings were 'usually classified as historical landscape, a type of painting traditionally placed a step above landscape painting and a step below history painting in the academic hierarchy of artistic genres' (Truettner and Wallach 79). In this series of paintings, the viewer can see that the relation between landscape and history is also uncoordinated. The series of *The Course of Empire* indicates the chain of human civilization, and 'the rise and fall of an empire'.

Cole created a crag as a 'landmark' (Ringe 29) as a reference to hold the whole design of his paintings. The problem is, the viewer can see the progress of human history in this series of paintings, but landscape does not 'contain' the ruin of the empire. The crag in the paintings is at a standstill, like an 'everlasting' (Ringe 30) landmark, which has its own uniqueness. As Ringe claims, Cooper and Cole shared in their works the 'specific parallels' (Ringe 26)—one is the landscape reference, the other is the 'illusion of the cyclical theory of history' (Ringe 27), as one can see in forms of both arts: verbal and visual.

Almost all the critics agree with the point, that Cole's landscape paintings illustrate the 'cyclical theory of history' (Ringe 165), especially the series of *The Course of Empire.*

And yet, there are two problems here. First of all, I do not see Cole's sense of history in a sort of 'cyclical order' (Ringe 165) in his paintings. Secondly, I wonder why landscape and history are still two separate entities in both Cooper's narrative and in Cole's painterly illustration. In other words, why Cooper's and Cole's landscape can stand outside of history? In the progress of history, why is American landscape not ruined by time in both art forms? What did Cooper and Cole intend to present through landscape?

In the nineteenth-century, American landscape was once the 'subject of speeches, magazine articles, and literary essays, and it dominated the consciousness of artists and writers who sought out the truly unique features of their country' (Asleson and Moore 4). For the first question I mentioned above, I think the 'cycle' of history does not indicate a sense of repetition or eternity. In *The Course of Empire*, the series show five stages of the 'growth and destruction of a great civilization' (Ringe 165). The reader can see that the last stage is 'a state roughly approximating its first rude beginnings'.

The 'cycle' is not real, because the ruin of the empire does not equal to its barbaric first stage. The 'cycle' simply cannot take us back to the initial stage of civilization or history. For the second question I mentioned above, it is really very bizarre to see a standstill—an unaltered landscape which refuses to contain the rise and fall of history. Actually, Cooper appreciated *The Course of Empire* very much. He thought that this series combined the 'feeling of beauty and sublimity, that denote genius. It is quite a new thing to see landscape painting raised to a level of the heroic, in historical compositions' (Cooper Letters 397). To me, landscape and history do not fit into each other quite well, since history is progressing and changing, how come landscape remains unaltered?

III. Landscape—History—Artists

As my writing goes on, it seems that I can figure out the answers for those two questions. Both Cooper and Cole wanted to express similar things, but only they used different forms of art: one used words, the other colors. The dialectical relation between landscape and history comes as such. First of all, both Cooper and Cole created a landmark, or, a reference to hold their artistic design, such as Gleen's Falls in *The Last of Mohicans* and the crag in *The Course of Empire*. Consequently, landscape is not merely a setting, but a subject. Secondly, the reader can see the uncoordinated tension between landscape and history. That is, landscape and history are two separate entities. Landscape does not contain the rise and fall of the empire, the alteration of history.

The tension comes from the uncoordinated relation between the changing history and the unaltered landscape. Synthesizing the first and the second points, I can see that landscape is a standpoint for both Cooper and Cole, in order to envision the progress of history. American landscape under their feet will not change, as it if is always there—showing the significance of their own present. Each moment, while they hold that standpoint in their mind, the progress of history seems to be approachable.

History, at that initial moment, fixed its eyes on them. Through landscape, history and the creative individuals meet up.

It is true that 'landscape' makes America unique. Cole himself was the one who 'began to reflect on the situation of the American landscape painter' (Truettner and Wallach 51). He thought that

> The painter of American scenery has indeed privileges superior to any other; all nature here is new to Art. No Tivili's [,] Terni's [,] Mount Blanc's, Plinlimmons, hackneyed & waterfalls feast his eyes with new delights, fill his port-folio with their features of beauty & magnificence and hallowed to his soul because they had been preserved untouched from the time of creation of his heaven-favoured pencil (Truettner and Wallach 51).

In other words, landscape is a subject, which American writers and painters want to identify with. Cooper and Cole took landscape as a standpoint to envision the progress of human history. They could envision the rise and fall of empires, races, and tribes. This standpoint of landscape is not going to move or change. Whenever the artists stand on the land, on the standpoint, each one of the moment is everlasting, is eternal.

When they stand on the standpoint and cast their eyes on history, history also fixes its eyes on them. As they approach history, at the same time, history also approaches them in their own minds. Landscape is the intersection of this meeting between history and the artist. The significance of the artistic vision lies on American landscape. Holding the landscape in mind, both Cooper and Cole can begin to 'historicize' (Jehlen 7) themselves as great figures of American literature and painting.

Works Cited

Asleson, Robyn, and Barbara Moore, eds. *Dialogue with Nature;
Landscape and Literature in Nineteenth-Century America.*
Washington, D.C.: The Corcoran Gallery of Art, 1985.

Cooper, James Fenimore. *The Last of the Mohicans.* Oxford:
Oxford University Press, 1998.

---. *The Letters and Journals of James Fenimore Cooper, Vol. 5.*
Ed. James Franklin Beard. Cambridge: Belknap of Harvard
University Press, 1968.

Jehlen, Myra. *American Incarnation.* Cambridge: Harvard
University Press, 1986.

Peck, H. Daniel, ed. *New Essays on* The Last of the Mohicans.
New York: Cambridge UP, 1992.

Franklin, Wayne. 'The Wilderness of Words in *The Last of the
Mohicans*'. Peck 25-46.

Martin, Terence. 'From Atrocity to Requiem: History in *The Last of the Mohicans*'. Peck 47-65.

Mc Willaims, John. *The Last of the Mohicans: Civil Savagery and Savage Civility*. New York: Twayne, 1995.

Nevius, Black. *Cooper's Landscapes: An Essay on the Picturesque Vision*. Berkeley: University of California Press, 1976.

Ringe, Donald A. *The Pictorial Mode: Space and Time in the Art of Bryant, Irving and Cooper*. Lexington: University Press of Kentucky, 1971.

---. 'James Fenimore Cooper and Thomas Cole: An Analogous Technique'. American Literature 30 (1958): 26.

Truettner, William H., and Alan Wallach, eds. *Thomas Cole: Landscape into History*. New Haven: Yale University Press, 1994.

· Chapter 6 ·

Self, Art, Fiction: *The Portrait of a Lady*

I want to explore the meanings and applications of the term 'the house of fiction' in Henry James's *The Portrait of a Lady* (1881). The structure of a fiction can be read as a construction through 'a number of possible windows', as James implied in the Preface of this novel (James, *Portrait* 8). The novelist's task is to express the individual's vision through these 'dissimilar' and 'disconnected' shapes and sizes of windows. In 'the house of fiction', some sees 'black' and some sees 'white'. Through James's standpoint, 'the consciousness of the artist' reveals the 'literary form' in a way that each individual's 'pair of eyes' opens a 'human scene'. Isabel Archer's consciousness is not an agent between what the author knows and what the reader may know. In the novel, James does not describe what Isabel knows.

Rather, he makes other characters to reveal her condition in the society, indicating the way in which things can be understood in life, between the self and the other, willing and circumstances, enclosure and openness.

Isabel Archer is Henry James's 'frail vessel' (Preface 12). Through this character, James's verbal portrait aims to represent a view of human relations, in this 'architecture' of the novel (Preface 13). As Leon Edel claimed in his *Henry James: A Life*, in the novel, 'James presents her to us as a young romantic with high notions of what life will bring her; he speaks of her "mixture of curiosity and fastidiousness, of vivacity and indifference," of her "combination of the desultory flame-like spirit and the eager and personal creature of her conditions" (Edel 258). Depicting Isabel's consciousness, James's 'literary monument' (Preface 13) reveals pictorial terms, in a way which a novelist can be seen as a painter, as James himself puts 'true [touches]' to his character 'for [his] canvas' (Preface 3). James's 'literary effort' (Preface 4) catches 'the image *en disponibilité*'—a 'free-floating image' of Isabel. As this 'fictive picture' (Preface 5) comes to express 'some

sincere experience' of James's impression of Venice, the artist
can also complete his vision of humanity.

I. The Dialectical Self

The structure of *The Portrait of A Lady*, I would argue,
is based on the changing characteristics of Isabel Archer. On
the surface, it may look like a typical 'female *Bildungsroman*'
(Jöttkandt 67), since the novel is about Isabel's returning to Mr
Osmond, revealing 'a developmental narrative during which
the hero undergoes a series of (usually painful) experiences that
teach her about herself and the world, resulting in an ethically
charged change in consciousness at the end' (Jöttkandt 67).
And yet, through different stages of Isabel's life in the fictional
world, James constructs his 'house of fiction', demonstrating
a way of seeing Isabel's consciousness, which plays the
centre of the subject' (Tóbin 261) of the novel, and appears
particularly clear in Chapter XLII of the novel via two earlier

stages—independence and marriage. In the first half of the novel, the reader can see that in order to look for the meaning of her life and to see the world through her own eyes, following her aunt Mrs Touchett, Isabel comes to Europe from Albany in America.

The novel turns into its second stage, when Mr Osmond expresses his love to Isabel in Chapter XXIX, as he finds himself 'in love with [Isabel]' (James, *Portrait* 335). Isabel loses her sense of independence at that moment, because her imagination will turn to something real, as she keeps 'silence', talking about nothing to no one, about how Mr Osmond 'occupied her thoughts' (James, *Portrait* 347). Although most critics would agree that Chapter XLII is a very obvious, so-called Jamesian revelation, as the night is a 'representation of [Isabel's] motionlessly *seeing*' (James, *Portrait* 17). And yet, I would argue, Isabel's vision about her true self is revealed in the very end of the novel, when she is kissed by Mr Goodwood. For Isabel, as James's narrator claims, Mr Goodwood's kiss

was like white lightening, a flash that spread, and spread

again, and stayed; and it was extraordinarily as if, while she took it, she felt each thing in his hard manhood that had least pleased her, each aggressive fact of his face, his figure, his presence, justified of its intense identity and made one with this act of possession. So had she heard of those wrecked and under water following a train of images before they sink. But when darkness returned she was free. She never looked about her: she only darted from the spot. There were lights in the windows of the house; they shone far across the lawn. In an extraordinarily short time—for the distance was considerable—she had moved through the darkness (for she saw nothing) and reached the door. Here only she paused. She looked all about her; she listened a little; then she put her hand on the latch. She had not known where to turn; but she knew now. There was a very straight path (James, *Portrait* 628).

This scene depicts the way in which James links the inner and the outer worlds through the perspective of a character. Here, the reader can only imagine what Isabel's path looks like, and where it leads to. It seems that Isabel's path is going to lead her to see what she really wants—to be able to make her own choice in life. James's narrator does not inform the reader what she would do after she goes back to Rome. Therefore, the novel itself cannot be seen as a properly ended text, only because all 'the events' seem to '[lead] to a conclusion' (Sontag 223). The ending of the novel looks like a flashback of memory, as Isabel's 'train of images' reminds her 'like a white lightening'. Mr Goodwood's kiss does not arouse the feeling of love in Isabel's consciousness. Rather, it reminds in her the dark consequences of her choices and decisions. Although marring to Mr Osmond is totally based on Isabel's free will, she has to face the reality that she has become his possession, 'in his hard manhood', as she is now feeling instantly in Mr Goodwood's arm. As Sarah Blackwood suggests, 'Isabel's body' is 'a form of thought itself', which is not only an agent of 'expressing emotion or thought' (Blackwood 275). Here Isabel's 'lips' (James, *Portrait* 627) feels the desire of her running away, since through Isabel's words, Mr Goodwood would not 'go away' (James, *Portrait* 627).

In 'the house of fiction', as James claims in the Preface of *The Portrait of a Lady*, through the 'window' of perception, every character has his or her own 'observation', 'impression' ('Preface' 8), and sometimes very different ways to approach and to make sense of what one sees. The way of seeing one's own self indicates one's relation to the external world. For example, Mme Merle is 'too perfectly the social animal that man and woman are supposed to have been intended to be', as she 'exist[s] only in her relations, direct or indirect, with her fellow mortals' (James, *Portrait* 213). She sees everything as a representation of the self, as everyone lives in his or her own 'shell'. If one wants to know about the self, one 'must take the shell into account' (James, *Portrait* 222). The self is a kind of 'spectacle', under a social 'representational scheme' (Marshall 268). As Mme Merle wonders, "What shall we call our 'self'? Where does it begin? where does it end? It overflows into everything that belongs to us—and then it flows back again" (James, *Preface* 223). The image of the self seems to be soft and uncertain, as it 'overflows into' the external objects, such as one's clothes. Mme Merle's perspective reinforces a self that can be recognised and can be caught, revealing James's aim of writing about 'the image *en disponibilité*'—a 'free-floating image' of Isabel, seen a changeable 'self-expression' (O'Connor 26).

For David M. Lubin, Mme Merle's and Isabel's ways of seeing the self represent different concepts of 'reality'. What Isabel sees is a core reality—the 'essence', a 'soul' (Lubin 132) which will not change through the external or material circumstances. Isabel would not think the same with Mme Merle's concept of the self. She is more like an 'idealist', rather than a 'realist' (Lubin 132) like Mme Merle. Her perception of the self is detached from the external objects. There is no direct relation between them, as the clothes cannot express the self. There seems to be a naked self, like an oyster without a shell, which exists as an isolated, pure self, in contrast with 'the envelope of social relations' (Boudreau 46). Marianna Torgovnick has claimed in *The Visual Arts, Pictorialism, and the Novel*, Jamesian 'impression' in the narrative can be read as an expression of 'visual perception', revealing 'Isabel's change' and 'ideological uses James makes of the visual arts in *The Portrait of a Lady*' (Torgovnick 163). I would suggest, James's painter-like vision as a way of perception shows the best in *The Ambassadors*. As Lambert Strether remembers the small landscape painting, which he failed to purchase in Boston, the French countryside became an Impressionist painting with 'a man who held the paddles and a lady, [...], with a pink parasol' (James, *Ambassadors* 309), indicating Strether's awareness of the love affair between Chad and Mme de Vionnet. Isabel's visual perception, on the other hand, is more about discovering her 'self'.

The development of Isabel's perception, as Patrick Fessenbecker has pointed out, reveals a desire of freedom 'toward a Kantian, ethical one, where an agent freely chooses her determined status' (Fessenbecker 75), in a way which one's own decisions or choices can be free from any ideologies, social conventions and judgments. To compare with Mme Merle's definition of the 'self', Isabel's self, as Viola Hopkins Winner defined, has the determination to 'transcend the limitations of the conventional, socially defined self' (Winner 97). In the context of the novel, the self of Isabel's would seem to be an imaginary one, aiming to form an illusion of self-reliance, which urges her to marry to Mr Osmond without considering other people's opinions.

For Mme Merle, Isabel is only 'the young American' girl (James, *Portrait* 194), because she can still 'feel' (James, *Portrait* 209) and can appreciate what she sees, before her point of view comes to represent Mr Osmond's, as a small corner of his garden, as his possession. The moment when Isabel meets Mme Merle, playing piano in the salon of Mr Touchette's house, can be seen as a turning point of Isabel's life. James's portraiture of Isabel's self shows a dialectical form. The piano music comes between two major silent period of her life. In the novel, the first silence starts from Chapter III when Isabel sits 'alone with a book', 'in her grandmother's old house in Albany'. At that time, she was a 'bright, alert, high-spirited, imaginative, pretty, bookish girl with a strong taste for independence, who has led a relatively secluded, permissive, protective life' (Friend 86-87). The second period of silence is in Chapter XLII, which is about Isabel's meditation and self knowledge, from the narrator's point of view. In that Chapter, the reader can see that everyone has his or her own 'window' (James, *Portrait* 462) to see things. From Isabel's perspective, she sees that Mr Osmond cannot 'live without' caring for the 'society'. Both of them have very different 'windows'—that is, very different 'ideas, such different associations and desires, to the same formulas' (James, *Portrait* 462). For example, Isabel's 'notion of the aristocratic life was simply the union of great knowledge with great liberty; the knowledge would give one a sense of duty and the liberty a sense of enjoyment'. And yet, Mr Osmond would think that all these things are a set of 'forms, a conscious, calculated attitude'—in one word, a 'tradition' (James, *Portrait* 462). But no matter what would happen, '[h]er mind was to be his—attached to his own like a small garden-plot to a deer-park' (James, *Portrait* 463), showing 'Unitarianism' which 'serve[s] James's purpose' (Bollinger 160). Isabel realises 'the truth'—not only the way in which Osmond and 'Madame Merle unconsciously and familiarly associated' (James, *Portrait* 467), but also the ugliness of Mr Osmond's characteristics, such as cynicism and egoism which 'lay hidden like a serpent in a bank of flowers' (James, *Portrait* 461). The 'truth' brings out Isabel's own feeling of

> terror with which she had taken the measure of her dwelling. Between those four walls she had lived ever since; they were to surround her for the rest of her life. It was the house of darkness, the house of dumbness, the house of suffocation. Osmond's beautiful mind gave it neither light nor air; Osmond's beautiful mind indeed seemed to peep down from a small high window and mock at her (James, *Portrait* 461).

Mr Osmond's 'beautiful mind'—loving arts, treating Isabel with a 'perfectly polite' manner (James, *Portrait* 461)—indicates a fake sense of 'liberty' (James, *Portrait* 461) which Isabel has. The real house Isabel lives in with Mr Osmond is as dark as her symbolic 'four walled room' (Benjamin 37)—her consciousness. Mr Osmond's politeness would not bring any light to Isabel's

perception. It would not make her see. Rather, it represents Mr
Osmond's male gaze, a tension in the house, a fear that Isabel
fears of losing her privacy and of being 'peep[ed] down from a
small high window and mock[ed] at' (James, *Portrait* 461). Mr
Goodwood's kiss somehow makes Isabel see the 'truth', as 'when
darkness returned she was free' (James, *Portrait* 627). Through
this kiss, Isabel sees the 'white lightening, a flash' shining
through her consciousness, paralleling 'lights in the windows of
the house' (James, *Portrait* 627). The dialectics of darkness and
light, silence and music, the unknown and the visual, truth and
imagination, comes to show this 'very straight path' of Isabel's
life—a path to home.

According to the ending of *The Portrait of a Lady*, the
reader can see that Isabel goes back to Rome. For many critics,
Isabel's going back to Rome means that she chooses to go back
to Mr Osmond. And yet, it is not clear that what Isabel will do,
after returning to Rome. It is very much unknown, that she will
be with Mr Osmond or not, as Henrietta suggests Mr Goodwood,
'just you wait' and see (James, *Portrait* 628). Isabel's self is

dialectic. Isabel desires her freedom from the very beginning. But only in the darkness she is free now to imagine. This also comes to show her way of seeing the self, which is very different from Mme Merle, as two opposite poles. At the end, Isabel's decision of going back to Rome also can be seen as a demonstration of freedom—the freedom of making choices, rather than giving 'the honor' (Niemtzow 378) to her married status. James's narrative stress is on Isabel's freedom to act and to decide. Her decision is made with her seeing and realising herself as an object, under the 'act of possession' (James, *Portrait* 627) physically by Mr Goodwood and mentally by Mr Osmond's gaze, and performing the 'act' of returning to Rome.

II. Art, Representation and Narration

Works of art can be seen as representations of the self. Human instinct is visualised as a form of fine arts. In *The Portrait of a Lady*, as the reader can see, Isabel senses the hidden history between Mme Merle and Osmond, when she sees the moment of their 'familiar silence' (James, *Portrait* 438). Mr Osmond 'was in a deep chair, leaning back and looking at [Mme Merle]'. The scene 'arrested' Isabel, because Osmond 'was sitting while Mme Merle stood' (James, *Portrait* 438). Since then, Isabel's feeling and her initial perception toward Mme Merle has changed, from an admirable friend to something as horrible as 'a walking picture' in Isabel's consciousness, which does not have a sense of being a complete human being. Mme Merle's 'extreme self-control' and her 'highly-cultivated' manner represent a 'firm surface, a sort of corselet of silver' (James, *Portrait* 431-432), as she 'had suppressed enthusiasm; […], she lived entirely by reason and by wisdom' (James, *Portrait* 432).

Isabel's feeling of horror comes, because of her realisation of Mme Merle's 'emotional and spiritual emptiness and her amorality' (Laird 645). Mme Merle can be seen only as a 'careful cultivation of the social and aesthetic modes of existence' (Laird 645). Apart from that appearance, there is not much inside her 'self'. James's narrator also describes Mr Osmond as a man, whose appearance 'was not handsome, but he was fine, as fine as one of the drawings in the long gallery above the bridge of the Uffizi' (James, *Portrait* 271). Again, on the surface, Mr Osmond looks like a person who has a great sense of aesthetics. He himself even looks like one of the fine drawings in the art gallery. And yet, Mr Osmond's personality shows exactly a sense of 'false aestheticism' (Stambaugh 502), as there is always an ugly truth, as something amoral or inhuman, hiding behind each painting-like impression.

Isabel's mind picture of Mme Merle has been externalised through her consciousness, visualising her fear. On the other hand, James's narrative also shows the reader a totally opposite pole, in a way which the dialectic relation between the inner and the outer worlds comes to synthesise Mr Rosier's vision of Isabel, as she comes 'out of the deep doorway' (James, *Portrait* 396). As Lotus Snow claimed, people around Isabel 'contribute their impressions of her' (Snow 315). Mr Rosier's appreciation and admiration can be visualised by seeing Isabel in a pictorial form, as she was dressed in black velvet; She looked high and splendid, [...], and yet oh so radiantly gentle! [...]. Mrs Osmond, at present, might well have gratified such tastes. The years had touched her only to enrich her; the flower of her youth had not faded, it only hung more quietly on its stem. [...]. Now, at all events, framed in the gilded door-way, she struck our young man as the picture of a gracious lady. (James, *Portrait* 396).

The verbal portrait of Isabel depicts how Isabel's self changes, from the American 'young lady' (James, *Portrait* 108) to an imaginary, probably also an Europeanised and an idealised lady, who is 'framed in the gilded door-way'. Isabel's image is like a work of art. Isabel's 'youth had not faded', as the real young lady Miss Pansy Osmond, Isabel's stepdaughter would show. James's 'use of framing technique' defines his 'pictorialism' (Hopkins 566), in a way which a subject has been described as a painting. The framed Isabel is an image with metaphorical meanings, in terms of the way to look at Isabel's self, between appearance and reality. As Ralph has asked Isabel for many times, 'Are you happy'? From the appearance of what she wears and how she looks—she looks perfectly fine, as young and as beautiful as before—just before her marriage. And yet, the 'frame' of James's verbal portrait reminds the reader Robert Browning's 'My Last Duchess', who is a beautiful lady but only serves as the property of her husband, as flat as an object 'painted on the wall' (Greenblatt 1255). Isabel becomes a pleasant object, for people and guests to watch, instead of being herself, as if she 'will never escape, she will last to the end' (McMaster 66).

The aim of *The Portrait of a Lady* is to represent the image of Isabel Archer. Through analysing James's writing technique, one can see the way in which he brings Isabel's self into focus. The relation between Isabel's consciousness and the social condition in the novel will come to define James's strategy, in terms of the logic behind the making of this verbal portrait of Isabel. Isabel's 'image *en disponibilité*'—a 'free-floating image' of Isabel is caught in James's 'house of fiction'. Many critics have been trying to pin that image down through a real portrait. For instance, Adeline R. Tintner in her 'The Art in the Fiction of Henry James', demonstrates 'a museum tour, for that is virtually what a trip through James's fiction turns out to be' (Tintner 285). A work of art can be used in writing, 'as a fruitful strategy for the construction of [James's] fiction' (Tintner 285). James's verbal portrait of Isabel reminds the reader 'a charming Constable' (James, *Portrait* 108)—which is one of the paintings Miss Henrietta Stackpole looks at 'in perfect silence' (James, *Portrait* 108).

Although the reader does not know which painting of Constable's that Ralph and Miss Stackpole see, I find Constable's *Portrait of a Lady* (about 1820, Tate Gallery, in Edwards, between 203 and 204) represents the image of James's Isabel. The young lady in the portrait is sitting on the grass, with a background of a huge column and a forest. She is sitting with 'a book of music' (Edwards 203) open on her knees. Her smile and her dress do not bring a sense of complexity, as Da Vinci's *Mona Lisa*. Rather, they show youth—an untouchable youth—a sense of freshness that Ralph and Miss Stackpole see in Isabel, in the initial stage of Isabel's coming to England, before she meets Mme Merle and listens to her piano play.

The Victorian realistic sense in this novel can also be read in architectural terms—namely, the houses in *The Portrait of a Lady*. For representing Isabel's consciousness, James makes the reader to see her surroundings in her life, linking the relation between the self and the society. In order to understand James's writing style and technique, it is worth it to examine why a common American girl such as Isabel herself, shall be 'doing' in 'an "architectural" competence' (James, *Portrait* 13), as the structure of a novel would show. In a love relation, Isabel's 'own consciousness' (James, *Portrait* 12) is important not only for Mr Osmond, but also for Ralph, for Mr Goodwood, and for Lord Warburton. James's 'architecture' of fiction aims to depict 'the view of [Isabel's] relation to those surrounding her' (James, *Portrait* 12). James explains his intensions with visual terms, creating 'a literary monument' through 'a plot of ground' with 'neat and careful and proportioned piles of bricks', which gives this literary monument a 'form' (James, *Portrait* 13).

James's literary realism is within an architectural form, as the reader can see 'the artful patience' in his composition in detail, when he

piled brick upon brick. The bricks, for the whole counting-over—putting for bricks little touches and inventions and enhancements by the way—affect me in truth as wellnigh innumerable and as ever so scrupulously fitted together and packed in. It is an effect of detail, of the minutest; though, if one were in this connection to say all, one would express the hope that the general, the ampler air of the modest monument still survives (James, *Portrait* 16).

This architecture of fiction presents the best James's own literary sense and style. Through all the efforts, the reader can have a picture of Isabel's image, as the centre of the novel. It is represented in two ways—one through her relations with men, in a way in which the string, her good female friend Henrietta Stackpole comes to suggest and to pin point the importance of these relations. On the other hand, the reader can also sense the image of Isabel when she is isolated from the others—most significantly, when she is alone in the library in the house in Albany and later in the drawing-room in Mr Osmond's house.

Following Ivan Turgenieff's method of creating 'the fictive picture' (James, *Portrait* 5), James also aims to depict his 'subject' within 'the chances, the complications of existence', and represents the subject in 'the right relations' (James, *Portrait* 5). In order to achieve this aim, Jamesian narrative technique comes to articulate human relations, in a way in which houses are used to represent the milieu and the character, as one can see in Mr Touchette's house and garden, in Osmond's house, and in Lord Warburton's house.

In the beginning of the novel, James depicts a pictorial view of Victorian 'sense of leisure'—an hour of 'the ceremony' of 'afternoon tea'—an 'innocent pastime' 'upon the lawn of an old English country-house' in a summer afternoon (James, *Portrait* 19). The 'red brick' house 'had a name and a history', (James, *Portrait* 20) indicating the owner Mr Touchette's successful and

honourable life. As Isabel first walks into the lawn to meet Mr
Touchette and Ralph, showing 'a great deal of confidence, both
in herself and in others' (James, *Portrait* 31), as if she can 'do
whatever' she wants (James, *Portrait* 97). Lord Warburton also
shows Isabel his house—which is a 'noble' house, 'as a castle in
a legend' (James, *Portrait* 97). Isabel likes the things she sees,
and yet, she does not feel comfortable to be herself. Rather, she
feels that she is 'quite in [her] aunt's hands' (James, *Portrait*
97). Mr Osmond's 'hill-top' shows his confidence in 'a soft
afternoon in the full maturity of Tuscan spring' (James, *Portrait*
277), when Isabel comes with Mme Merle, to visit him, his
sister Countess Gemini and his daughter Pancy. Osmond's villa
is a 'principle' and a very 'imposing object' (James, *Portrait*
277). It is protected by the Roman Gate, high walls, and the
'blank superstructure' and 'the fine clear arch' (James, *Portrait*
277). It is a place 'once you were in, you would need an act of
energy to get out' (James, *Portrait* 277). Isabel feels that 'there
is something in the air, in her general impression of things'
(James, *Portrait* 279). In order to observe, she feels that she

does not need 'to put herself forward', to 'try to understand—she would not simply utter graceful platitudes' (James, *Portrait* 279). Architectural structures come to represent Isabel's different states of mind. It is exactly James's own style, in a way in which the reader can see the image of Isabel from different aspects, through the houses she is in.

III. Jamesian Style

As James's close writer friend Edith Wharton has pointed out, James's 'genius' (Wharton 914, 915, 922 and 932) can be seen through his 'keenness of perception' (Wharton 920) and his 'experiments in technique and style' (Wharton 929) of fictional writing. Among James's short fictions and novels, 'Daisy Miller' and *The Portrait of a Lady* are Wharton's favorite, because they indirectly show dramatic events of the mind. Although James's portrait of perception achieves its mature stage, such as the lack of action and plot as the reader can see in *The Ambassadors*,

James's writing style seems to stick to 'a predestined design, and design, in his strict geometrical sense', which for Wharton is 'one of the least important things in fiction' (Wharton 926). Certainly, Wharton's observation indicates Jamesian sensibility, which comes to reveal the form of the novel in artistic, architectural, or geometrical senses.

In *The Portrait of a Lady*, one can see James's use of 'the language of painting' (Sweeney 11) in his fiction, giving meanings to visual objects through words, constructing a fictional world of images and a system of signs through depicting the interaction between the inner and the outer worlds. Isabel's fear is the key mood of the novel, expressing through her reaction to things happened, seen from the outside.

The definition of the writing style of James's own is difficult to be seen via only one novel. And yet, *The Portrait of a Lady* somehow catches the essence of James's concept of making fiction as a form of 'the *fine* arts' (James, 'The Art of Fiction' 6), in order to depict 'the truth' of the artist's own (James, 'The Art of Fiction' 5). James's novel should be read as painting in words, because as a writer, he would not agree with the idea that a painting and a novel can represent different things, such as 'the picture is reality, so the novel is history' (James, 'The Art of Fiction' 5). For James, a writer's aim of writing a fiction is to make it 'represent life' (James, 'The Art of Fiction' 5), as one can see the same aim on the canvas of a painter. As Leon Edel pointed out in his 'Henry James as an Art Critic', if a viewer can see the inner and the external realities in both a painting and a novel, then somehow, a 'Cézanne' and a 'Flaubert' are both 'in a manner of speaking, the same thing' (Edel 6).

Works Cited

Baldick, Chris. *Oxford Dictionary of Literary Terms*. Oxford: Oxford UP, 2008.

Benjamin, Walter. *Charles Baudelaire: A Lyric Poet in the Era of High Capitalism*. Trans. Harry Zohn. London: NLB, 1973.

Blackwood, Sarah. "Isabel Archer's Body". *The Henry James Review* 31.3 (2010): 271-279.

Bollinger, Laurel. "'Poor Isabel, who had never been able to Understand Unitarianism!'": Denominational Identity and Moral Character in Henry James's *The Portrait of a Lady*'. *The Henry James Review* 32.2 (2011): 160-177.

Boudreau, Kirstin. '*Is* the World Then So Narrow? Feminist Cinematic adaptations of Hawthorne and James'. *The Henry James Review* 21.1 (2000): 43-53.

Edel, Leon. 'Henry James as an Art Critic'. *American Art Journal* 6.2 (1974): 4-14.

---. *Henry James: A Life*. New York: Harper & Row, 1985.

Edwards, Ralph. 'A Portrait by John Constable at the Tate Gallery'. *The Burlington Magazine for Connoisseurs* 74.434 (1939): 202-204.

Fessenbecker, Patrick. 'Freedom, Self-Obligation, and Selfhood in Henry James'. *Nineteenth-Century Literature* 66.1 (2011): 69-95.

Friend, Joseph H. 'The Structure of *The Portrait of a Lady*'. *Nineteenth-Century Fiction* 20.1 (1965): 85-95.

Greenblatt, Stephen, ed. *The Norton Anthology of English Literature, Volume 2*. New York: W. W. Norton, 2006.

Hopkins, Viola. *PMLA* 76.5 (1961): 561-574.

James, Henry. *The Art of Fiction and Other Essays*. New York: Oxford UP, 1948.

---. *The Ambassadors*. Ed. S. P. Rosenbaum. New York: W. W. Norton, 1994.

---. Preface. Oxford: Oxford UP, 1998.

---. *The Portrait of a Lady*. Oxford: Oxford UP, 1998.

Jöttkandt, Sigi. 'Portrait of an Act: Aesthetics and Ethics in *The Portrait of a Lady*'. *The Henry James Review* 25.1 (2004): 67-86.

Laird, J. T. 'Cracks in Previous Objects: Aestheticism and Humanity in *The Portrait of a Lady*'. *American Literature* 52.4 (1981): 643-648.

Lubin, David M. *Act of Portrayal: Eakins, Sargent, James*. New Haven: Yale UP, 1985.

Marshall, Gail. 'Performances in *The Portrait of a Lady*'. *The Henry James Review* 31.3 (2010): 264-270.

McMaster, Juliet. 'The Portrait of Isabel Archer'. *American Literature* 45.1 (1973): 50-66.

Niemtzow, Annette. 'Marriage and the New Woman in *The Portrait of a Lady*'. *American Literature* 47.3 (1975): 377-395.

O'Conner, Dennis L. 'Intimacy and Spectatorship in *The Portrait of a Lady*'. *The Henry James Review* 2.1 (1980): 25-35.

Sontag, Susan. *At the Same Time: Essays and Speeches.* Ed. Paolo Dilonardo and Anne Jump. London: Hamish Hamilton, 2007.

Snow, Lotus. '"The Disconcerting Poetry of Mary Temple": A Comparison of the Imagery of *The Portrait of a Lady* and *The Wings of the Dove*'. *The New England Quarterly* 31.3 (1958): 312-339.

Sweeney, John L. Introduction. *The Painter's Eye.* By Henry James. Madison: The U of Wisconsin P, 1989.

Tintner, Adeline R. 'The Art in the Fiction of Henry James'. *A Companion to Henry James Studies.* Ed. Daniel Mark Fogel. London: Greenwood, 1993.

Tóbin, Colm. 'A Death, a Book, an Apartment: *The Portrait of a Lady*'. *The Henry James Review* 30.3 (2009): 260-265.

Wharton, Edith. *Novellas and Other Writings.* New York: The Library of America, 1990.

Winner, Viola Hopkins. *Henry James and the Visual Arts.* Charlottesville: The UP of Virginia, 1970.

· Chapter 7 ·

London and Crisis
in Henry James's *The Awkward Age*

I read Henry James's *The Awkward Age* (1899), in order
to seek the answers of this essential question: Why does James
choose dialogues to represent life in London? Through a close
reading of the novel itself, I would argue that language creates
an outer form of the reality, by dialogues, performances and
acts. Although *The Awkward Age* is a work which marks James's
literary practice of a form of a novel; however, the inner form
of the reality, such as a character's consciousness or thought, is
totally missing. In this novel, it seems that the more one says,
the less one knows. The more James aims to depict the reality,
the more he comes to avoid description. I would argue that
this writing technique can be understood as a Jamesian 'crisis'

(Preface xxx) of textual practice, representing an anti-realism narrative form. Language reveals a crisis, in a way which language not only creates confusions, but also brings illusions. It shows exactly the opposite of what is real. Even Zola's novel appears in the end of the novel, as an object which makes Nanda feels superior. And yet, Nanda needs to feel superior, because she is not a heroine. She has her 'domestic difficulties and a cage in her window' (James, *Awkward* 332). These things suggest virtue for a young girl, so that she can easily miss 'the great wicked city, the wonderful London sky and the monuments looming through' (James, *Awkward* 332).

I. Introduction

To write about Henry James's *The Awkward Age*, I ask myself: How shall I start? Where shall I begin with? The style of this novel is quite unusual, because it 'has often been described as almost entirely in dialogue' (Poole 10). And yet, it does not help, even if the reader paid much attention to the dialogue itself—identifying problems such as who says what, to whom, and what it is all about. The sense of awkwardness is revealed, because Nanda 'already knows too much' (James, *Awkward* 367). No matter what that means, she is not as innocent as a virgin. Ironically, to get married seems to be the only way that she can be out of that situation. But since she is not virgin-like pure, no one will be able to marry her.

Through writing, I will be able to seek the answers of this essential question: Why does James choose dialogues to represent the reality of life in London? Through a close reading of the novel itself, I would argue that language creates an outer form of the reality, by dialogues, performances and acts. *The Awkward Age* is a work which marks James's literary practice of a form of a novel. However, the inner form of the reality, such as a character's consciousness or thoughts, in this respect, is not very easy to define.

II. James's Realism

The essential question is: what kind of reality that *The Awkward Age* comes to unfold? James's aim of using dialogues and gestures to show a sense of the real: things happen in London. However, as far as the reader can see, language not only creates confusions, but also brings illusions. It shows exactly the opposite of what is real. As when Mr Longdon looks at Nanda's photograph in the room, he says to Vanderback that 'Nanda isn't so pretty' (James, *Awkward* 15). The reader can find out that for Mr Longdon, Nanda is less pretty when comparing to her grandmother. But the reader cannot see any concrete descriptions of what the photograph looks like, what Nanda looks like, or what Nanda's grandmother looks like. Language here is like an image, which comes in a way to cover an inner reality—what is going on in Mr Longdon's mind? What makes him to say things like that?

In this novel, it seems that the more one says, the less one knows. The more James aims to depict the reality, the more he comes to avoid description. I would argue that this writing technique can be understood as a Jamesian 'crisis' (Preface xxx) of textual practice, representing an anti-realism narrative form. Even Zola's novel (although the reader cannot know which one) appears in the end of the novel, as an object which makes Nanda feels superior. And yet, Nanda needs to feel superior, because she is not a heroine. She has her 'domestic difficulties and a cage in her window' (James, *Awkward* 332), as James depicts. These 'domestic difficulties' somehow suggest virtue for a young girl, so that she can easily miss 'the great wicked city, the wonderful London sky and the monuments looming through' (James, *Awkward* 332).

In *Henry James, Women and Realism*, Victoria Coulson defines James's narrative form of the novel as one of the representations of the 'ambivalent realists', namely among Alice James, Constance Fenimore Woolson and Edith Wharton. As Coulson argues, if the reader considers the novel form as a kind of textual experiment, one can come up with a conclusion that

> not all nineteenth-century realisms are ambivalent; or
> at least, not all are as *fundamentally* equivocal as is this
> mode—and, at the same time, its aesthetic and cultural
> centrality: this is a very significant 'dialect' within the
> broader linguistic range of nineteenth-century narrative
> representation, and it adumbrates an uneasy apprehension
> of the semiotic revolutions to come' (Coulson 11).

James's realism is somehow 'ambivalent', because in *The Awkward Age*, language and dialogue do not help the reader to make sense of the reality—that is, 'what crisis created, what issue found' (Preface xxxii) in the very literary text. Language fails to deliver the meaning of things. As the reader can see, the whole novel is a process of information exchange through language. This form of exchange is informal, as London gossip is 'the socially sanctioned transfer of information from 'friend' to 'friend' (Seligson 71). And yet, the textual practice is ambivalent, because it is really problematic, when James intends to apply a theatrical method to the form of the novel. As David Kurnick points out, James's 'fictional world-making' seems to be a sort of 'performance', showing a play that 'we have not been invited' (Kurnick 113).

III. Crisis

The crisis of James's London society is that, as the reader can see, through the intensity of language, gesture and acting, every character in the novel is looking for a self-conscious freedom, even the reader does not know what exactly happened, only through reading. It does not matter who said what. The meaning of representing a crisis in this way is that Nanda suffers from her 'compromise' (Preface xxxv). Nanda's being around that social circle is exactly the very force of the little circle's freedom of speech.

The Awkward Age is constructed by ten Books. Each one

of them can be seen as a verbal portrait of the character in *The Awkward Age*—starting from Lady Julia in Book I, and followed by Little Aggie, Mr Longdon, Mr Cashmore, The Duchess in Book V, Mrs Brook, Mitchy, Tishy Grendon in Book VIII, Vanderbank and the last but not the least Nanda in Book X.

Stuart Culver, in his article 'Censorship and Intimacy: Awkwardness in *The Awkward Age*', points out that 'by writing a novel whose subject is dialogue entirely in dialogue, James has collapsed the distinction between subject and treatment, intension and form' (Culver 376). Culver's point sharply reveals the way in which the verbal form of the conversations in the drawing-room 'has come to stand as a substitute for truth' (Culver 376). For *The Awkward Age*, my reading does not focus on finding out what is the truth. Rather, I would argue, the crisis of the novel form stands in the process of representation, showing a gap between what things should be and misunderstanding, between reality and mis-representation.

James's novel shows a process of representation. And yet, the question is, how can this process be understood through reading the novel? In *The Awkward Age*, James's literary technique comes to show this process through words and conversations. Visual impressions come to represent knowledge in London, including observations and impressions of a person.

Photographic images are also very important. In this novel, a photograph shows not only a visual reality—the way Little Aggie looks like, but also James's verbal abstraction such as observations, memories and conversations which comes to be a contrast to a photographic reality. For instance, when Vanderbank and Mr Longdon have a conversation in a room, Van's observation of Mr Longdon makes him feel that he does not mean what he says. The 'small photograph' (James, *Awkward* 10) on the table shows that Little Aggie '*is* extremely pretty—with extraordinary red hair and a complexion to match; great rarities', as far as Van can see, 'in that race and latitude' (James, *Awkward* 10). Young girls give their own photos to friends as gifts, to show how much they appreciate their 'friendship' (James, *Awkward* 13). And yet, ironically, the reality that one can see from Van's perspective is that there is no such thing as 'friendship' in London life, because there are only 'sociable' elements rather than real feelings. Van himself has doubts to see 'the existence of friendship in big societies—in great towns and great crowds'. In fact, for him, friendship is like 'a plant that takes time and space and air; and London society is a huge "squash", as [people in London] elegantly call it—an elbowing, pushing, perspiring, chattering mob' (James, *Awkward* 13).

Vanderbank also has another photograph 'beside the lamp', which is a 'present' from Nanda herself, framed in 'glazed white wood' (James, *Awkward* 10 - 11). Both young girls, about eighteen, are as 'charming' as 'innocent lambs' (James, *Awkward* 11). The 'horror' is that Mrs Brookenham, Nanda's mother, treats her as if she was 'only sixteen' (James, *Awkward* 12). Little Aggie is also trapped in a small circle, which involves only four people—Dr Beltram, Aggie's aunt the Duchess, a governess Miss Merriman, and a nurse who is also an old maid, Gelsomina (James, *Awkward* 160).

Mr Longdon's tears suggest that Nanda is not as beautiful as his lover Lady Julia—who is Nanda's grandmother. The reader cannot see if Nanda is really less beautiful in that photograph. And yet, Mr Longdon's feeling and memory show the reader the reality that one perceived.

IV. James's London of the 1890s

The Awkward Age is not just another London novel. Through a 'forty-year association' with the capital of the Victorian Age, as John Kimmey argues in his *Henry James and London*, the reader can see James's 'shifting views of London', as 'the city changes in James's fiction' and 'his fiction changes with the city' (Kimmey ix). I would argue, London can be seen as a stage, which comes to provide the space for the drama of language through an Ibsenian theatrical realism, as James refers to *A Doll's House* in his Preface (xlii), showing James's path to modernity and its dual form of seeing reality. On the one hand, the drama of language highlights the importance of acting and performing, such as a character's gaze and observation toward another character. On the other hand, through reading a drama on paper, with a form of the novel, it seems that James tries to give his readers a space to have their own impressions, instead of describing psychological realism through a central character, as Strether's 'process of vision' (James, *Ambassadors* 2) in *The Ambassadors* would show.

The *Awkward Age* comes to '[sum] up certain aspects of the city observed during the period' (Kimmey 132) of the 1890s, as John Kimmey maintains. The talk within a small society highlights the importance of 'friends' and 'family', and yet, with a focus of 'scandals' and 'personal problems' (Kimmey 112). In the novel, Nanda's mother appears to be very sociable, looking younger than her age. Mrs Brookenham likes Vanderbank. However, her daughter Nanda quite likes him too. As a young girl, Nanda's crisis is that she lives in a 'hypocritical and cynical society of her mother' (Kimmey 132).

London, as a scope of the writing in Henry James's *The Awkward Age*, plays its own significant role, in a way which James's struggle of literary form reinforces the heroine Nanda's personal struggle. Through showing Nanda's crisis and unease in her life in London, James dramatically creates a new way to rewrite Victorian realism, aiming to depict a complex of social relations with a narrative form, in which multiple points of view come to draw 'the real things', indicating 'the true elements of any tension and true facts of any crisis' (Preface xxxiii) about women, with different references and a 'mathematically right' logic (Preface xliii), embracing the characteristics of London 'with a strong impression' (Preface xliv).

Nanda's crisis was created within a specific London social circle. For James, a writer cannot write about the complications of human relation and impressions of a person with an isolated form, which may happen to look like, in a painter's eye, 'a sharp black line, to frame in the square, the circle, the charming oval, that helps any arrangement of objects to become a picture' (Preface xxxii). *The Awkward Age* is about an impression of this particular social circle, which is 'richly sophisticated' (Preface xxxii). When writing about this small social circle, James turns the city of London into 'a deep warm jungle' (Preface xxxii) as in characters' dialogues, creating an impression of London of his own.

The concept of beauty in London—especially a kind of 'staring, glaring, obvious, knock-down beauty' (James, *Awkward* 17), as James's character Vanderbank points out while talking to Mr Longdon, is

> as plain as a poster on a wall, an advertisement of soap or whisky, something that speaks to the crowd and crosses the foot-lights, fetches such a price in the market that the absence of it, for a woman with a girl to marry, inspires endless terrors and constitutes for the wretched pair—to speak of mother and daughter alone—a sort of social bankruptcy. London does not love the latent or the lurking, has neither time, nor taste, nor sense for anything less discernible than the red flag in front of the steam-roller. It wants cash over the counter and letters ten feet high (James, *Awkward* 17).

A girl's appearance and the way in which people in London society see her are very important, especially when Nanda's mother Mrs Brookenham thinks that her daughter, in her young age of eighteen or nineteen years old, should be ready to get married. The way people see beauty is, unfortunately, as shallow as 'a poster on the wall'. Women are looked at, as objects in the market for sale, just like 'soap or whiskey'. The essential question is, what can Nanda or her mother do, to promote herself and to make herself look better, since people in London do not have 'time', 'sense' or 'taste' to see through the appearance of things? Nanda is like her grandmother Lady Julia, but only 'less pretty' (James, *Awkward* 16). People will not want to know her more, since Nanda's beauty is not that sort of impressive one, as London society is used to. Since her look cannot be promoted, as the way in which advertisement works, 'what will she able to do for herself' (James, *Awkward* 17)? Nanda's mother Mrs Brookenham knows about that. Mrs Brook likes Vanderbank a lot. Maybe that is the reason why she looks at the city of London in a similar way as his. In a conversation between Mrs

Brookenham and Mr Cashmore, she also makes comments on her impression of London, as women in the city like to dress up. People in London will like to see a young lady like her daughter Nanda to '[show] things' (James, *Awkward* 111)—just 'as some fine tourist region shows the placards in the fields and the posters on the rocks' (James, *Awkward* 111).

Friendship is like a plant, which needs 'time', 'space' and 'air' (James, *Awkward* 13) to grow. Vanderbank's view shows that it is difficult to believe 'in the existence of friendship in big cities', because London society is like a big 'squash', which is like 'an elbowing, pushing, perspiring, chattering mob' (James, *Awkward* 13). To be able to survive, Nanda definitely needs a group of people who truly love her and who want to protect her. According to Vanderbank's observation, and Mr Longdon's insight, they both believe that there is 'something' in each other's mind, that 'soft human spot' in which they can relate to each other, 'to have a real affinity' (James, *Awkward* 22). The reader can learn that Mr Longdon used to have a relation with Vanderbank's mother, right before his real love of life, Lady

Julia, got married. Mr Longdon says to Vanderbank twice 'good night, good night', both on page twenty and on page twenty-four of the novel, trying to avoid more questions from Vanderbank. For Mr Longdon himself, his 'deep memories' (James, *Awkward* 21) of youth and love seem to construct a wall as such—for the 'poster' to be put on. Although he considers himself as 'old-fashioned and narrow and dull', as a man had lived 'in a hole', who is 'not a man of the world', still, what Vanderbank sees in him is a 'delightful' and 'wonderful' quality (James, *Awkward* 23).

Mrs Brookenham, 'the virtuous English mother' (James, *Awkward* 41), is having a talk with Jane, the Duchess. Both of them are wondering, for their daughters Nadna and Aggie, the quality for a girl to be married. Are young men of Nanda and Aggie, still 'looking for smart, safe, sensible English girls' (James, *Awkward* 41) to get married? Both mothers think that an unmarried girl is very 'unfortunate' (James, *Awkward* 38), as if to be married shall be a fortunate thing which could happen to a young girl. Again, both mothers, through their dialogues, support each other to consider what kind of men is 'good enough' (James, *Awkward* 41) for their girls—it can be the type of Mitchy (Mr Mitchett), for instance, 'the grandson of a grasshopper' (James, *Awkward* 41). Or, nevertheless, Mr Vanderbank can also be a good candidate, but no one knows what his ideas about marriage are.

V. Conclusion

James knows what he is doing. He knows that in *The Awkward Age*, he 'encounter[s] none the "history" of which embodies a greater number of curious truths—or of truths at least by which [he] found contemplation more enlivened' (Preface xxix). The whole textual practice is 'a trick of looking dead if not buried'. James 'almost throbs with ecstasy when, on an anxious review, the flush of life re-appears' (Preface xxix-xxx). The novel itself, on the surface, may look like a total failure, since it does not fit in the typical sense of nineteenth-century realism.

The novel does not show the reality of the external world, say, the value of 'absolute realism' (Kimmey 16) as literary 'art's mimetic capacity' (Byerly 1), as a character's walking through the city of London. The novel also does not show an 'inner reality' (Byerly 60) of a character's consciousness, as the reader may expect to see in the Jamesian fictional narrative form. And yet, I would argue, through dialogues, the novel implies 'the awkward age' (Preface xxxiv) of the society, in a way which the 'awkwardness' is 'so morally well-meant and so intellectually helpless' (Preface xxxiv). The city of London has been simplified only through '"good" talk' (Preface xxxiv).

The Awkward Age seems to reveal such a crisis of writing—on the one hand, realism should be dead and be buried. And yet, James is trying to give the 'freedom' of speech to his characters, in order to develop the 'charm' of 'modernity', in the sense of 'frankness and ease' (Preface xxxiii). James does not intend to cover any 'ugly matters' of London through 'some rude simplification' of dialogues. The purpose of writing a novel is not to identify a problem, a 'situation', or 'any tension', or 'any crisis' (Preface xxxiii). The charm of modernity hides itself in the ease of talking. As for James, [t]here are more things in London, […] than anywhere in the world', to be talked about (Preface xxxv), even the ease of a 'morally well-meant' dialogue shows a social condition of 'intellectually helpless'.

Works Cited

Byerly, Alison. *Realism, Representation, and the arts in Nineteenth-Century Literature.* Cambridge: Cambridge UP, 1997.

Coulson, Victoria. *Henry James, Women and Realism.* Cambridge: Cambridge UP, 2007.

Culver, Stuart. 'Censorship and Intimacy: Awkwardness in *The Awkward Age*'. *ELH* 48.2 (1981): 368-386.

James, Henry. *The Awkward Age* (1899). Oxford: Oxford UP, 1999.

---. *The Ambassadors.* 1903. Ed. S. P. Rosenbaum. New York: Norton, 1994.

Poole, Adrian. 'Nanda's Smile: Teaching James and the Sense of Humor'. *The Henry James Review* 25.1 (2004): 4-18.

Kimmey, John. *Henry James and London.* New York: Peter Lang, 1991.

Kurnick, David. '"Horrible Impossible": Henry James's Awkward Stage'. *The Henry James Review* 26.2 (2005): 109-129.

Seligson, Judith. 'Visual Intertextuality: Drawing Comparisons in *The Wings of the Dove*'. *The Henry James Review* 31.1 (2010): 68-84.

· Chapter 8 ·

The Flâneur's Gaze and the Dialectical Representation of London: Using Woolf's "Street Haunting" as an Example

"But what defines human as opposed to animal desire is that its realization must entail an interaction which is the basis of history."

-Martin Jay, 'Lacan, Althusser, and the Specular Subject
of Ideology' (Jay, Downcast Eyes 345 - 346).

I. The Flâneur and Urban Visual Experience

I want to focus on literary representation of London. This theme invites the viewer to pay special attention to visual, spatial and pictorial motifs in textual elements—which have been constructed by narrative, verbal coded signs, and literary imaginary sequences. I would like to construct the representation of London in terms of what the flâneur sees and what he thinks. The function of mapping the representation of London is to make us see how London is visually and ideologically constructed in literary texts. The term "dialectical" has been used to indicate two levels of representation. Firstly, the dialectical power between ideology and social practice. Secondly, that power reveals the flâneur's dual vision: ideology and imagery.

The observational vision links the city, the external visual world, and public and social spheres with the viewer's

· Chapter 8 ·
The Flâneur's Gaze and the Dialectical Representation of London:
Using Woolf's "Street Haunting" as an Example

inwardness. The observational vision turns the external visual world into an inward, internalized and imaginary mapping process. 'Inward mapping is a thinking process. This thinking process is the operation of consciousness—the operation of the core self. Through this thinking process, the flâneur is able to turn the external visual world and the city space into his private four walls room or home' (Benjamin 37). These four walls room and home are metaphors of the flâneur's core self; they are references of the inwardness. This inward mapping process is a process of investigation of the city space with a psychological detachment. The flâneur walks in the city space to search for visual signs. These signifiers will be constructed as a new and critical picture to the public sphere, a place for displaying ideology in the capitalist system (Habermas 123).

The dialectic of the public sphere comes from conflicts among social classes and different social typifications and physiology—types of people, such as the flâneur, the blasé, the poor and so forth. Conflicts among social classes make the public sphere a ground for displaying ideologies. The flâneur's milieu is combined with two external visual elements—the labyrinth of the city itself and types of people. The flâneur is reading, observing and mapping the 'impression' of the milieu—the unique, the sensational, the picturesque. The 'imaginary mapping' process is the flâneur's way of seeing the labyrinth of the city as 'visual signs'—clues, fragments, signifiers, small details, momentary shocks. Through the imaginary mapping process, the flâneur is able to turn these signs into a re-presentation, a re-construction and a re-production of a literary text. This literary text is an expression of the essence of the city and the crowd.

The gaze of the flâneur—the spectator's vision—is an effective methodology for social, political, economic and cultural studies. For instance, with an eye of the flâneur, Walter Benjamin saw the arcade as a crucial image of nineteenth-century Paris. The arcade's early form of industrial luxury indicates the decay of his era, indicating mass production, consumption and the wish-image of the bourgeoisie. The flâneur's vision is useful to examine the 'everyday capitalist life' in the urban space—the rapid transformation of daily life, the experience of

· Chapter 8 ·
The Flâneur's Gaze and the Dialectical Representation of London:
Using Woolf's "Street Haunting" as an Example

modernization, the fashionable, and the 'New'. The flâneur's vision is somehow the manifesto of modernity.

II. The Dialectical Representation of the City

There are three features in the dialectical representation in terms of the observational vision of the flâneur—(1) Thesis: Ideology, (2) Anti-thesis: Social Practice, (3) Synthesis: Critical awakening and perception. Ideology is a conceptual formation. The flâneur's imaginary mapping process is a representation of ideology. Social practice, on the other hand, is the practice of ideology in 'the Real'—the realistic and material aspect of things. Critical awakening is a way of interpreting a social phenomenon. The interpretation synthesizes both ideological and social practical aspects in representation, with a form of literary text or a work of art.

Globalization is not only a phenomenon, but also a representation of ideology—a collective consciousness, a 'belief' (Marx and Engels 29). Under this ideological framework, people believe that they can earn more money from capitalism. For instance, the idea of 'free market' is a representation of ideology, which has been created by capitalism. But when this ideology has been put into 'social practice', such as the immigration of labour, we can see that issues such as "struggles" among social classes, ethnic and political groups make this 'ideology' looks problematic. The dialectics between ideology and social practice gives us a space of critique—to synthesize both sides to achieve a critical awakening. Critical awakening and perception indicate a way of interpretation and recognition. Also, this interpretation and recognition will be 'materialized' as the re-production and the re-presentation of literary text, in terms of social practice.

Through the observational eye of the flâneur, Paris is 'a city of signs' in Benjamin's text. However, the motive of the flâneur is from Poe's 'Man of the Crowd' of London. I will use this motive to see literary and visual representations of London. The critical perspective of the flâneur reveals the invisible text of the city. This invisible text is the 'imaginary psychological landscape' in Virginia Woolf's writing. It is the dialectical

· Chapter 8 ·
The Flâneur's Gaze and the Dialectical Representation of London:
Using Woolf's "Street Haunting" as an Example

representation of the city space—the dynamic powers of ideology and social practice. Through the act of gaze, the flâneur is able to transform the seductive visual objects into representations—the (re)production of a literary text in the social context.

III. Dialectical Representation of London: "Street Haunting"

Ideology and imagery are dialectical. The 'over-lapping' of these two constructs two modes of representation of London in the literary form. London becomes a market and an impression. In Virginia Woolf's literary text, we can see the way in which ideology and imagery as two dialectical powers work hand in hand, revealing the relationship between an individual and the social milieu he or she lives in. Woolf's 'Street Haunting: A London Adventure' is a good example.

We can read 'Street Haunting: A London Adventure' via the vision of the flâneur. It is a dual vision of ideology and imagery.

The narrator of 'Street Haunting' walks on the street of London. This narrator explores and observes street scenes of London on the way of buying a pencil. This literary text begins with an individual need—the act of consumption for a commodity. This narrator is a spectator, a consumer, a walker and a producer, who produces 'Street Haunting: A London Adventure', in terms of social practice.

In this text, a world of commodity has been revealed, such as a pencil, a cup of coffee in the coffee shop and so forth. A commodity an 'every-day thing' (Marx 81). Capitalism dominates the market in the city space. It makes a city an exchange network. The structure of this exchange network is based on 'modes of production'—say, to produce a pencil to sell. Someone buys this pencil to write, to publish a book, and to sell this book. In 'Street Haunting', we can see different exchange modes. For instance, 'the melancholy Englishman' exchanges 'the secret of his soul' with cups of coffee and iron tables in the coffee shop, 'as travelers do' (Woolf 481). It is an example of how the exchange network activates in the context of social consumption. An individual buy a cup of coffee via money. He sits

· Chapter 8 ·
The Flâneur's Gaze and the Dialectical Representation of London:
Using Woolf's "Street Haunting" as an Example

in the shop and drinks that cup of coffee. Then he exchanges his secret in mind with that cup of coffee—it is another example of the process of thinking, consideration and the operation of the inward gaze. The mode of production and the exchange construct the mode of representation in the context of metropolitan modernity. London, in this literary text, has been represented as a 'market'.

London is a world of commodity. Commodities are visual objects. Here I would like to evaluate and to develop Marx's theory of commodity fetishism in *Capital* from the economic level to a symbolic level. In this symbolic realm, 'commodity' is the exchange medium. The exchange of commodities reveals relationships among people. In the economic level, money is the medium for having exchange activities. Money is the symbolic token, which makes the act of consumption happen. In Marx's logic of 'commodity fetishism', the consumer buys commodity via money.

However, the consumer does not know who produces the commodity. There is no real connection or relationship between the producer and the consumer. Money is the medium, which keeps the network of social consumption working. The mode of production, consumption and money construct the social relationship between the consumer and the producer. There is an overlap between Marxism and Psycho-analysis. The term 'commodity fetishism' somehow reveals this overlap. The psycho-analytical aspect of using the term 'fetish' indicates the ritual function of a commodity in terms of social practice:

Marx adapts the term 'fetish' from its anthropological definition as an object believed to procure for its owner the services of a spirit lodged within it, an object regarded with irrational reverence. Etymologically, 'fetish' is derived from the Portuguese *feitico* meaning magic, a name subsequently given Portuguese traders to the cult objects of West Africa. (See the Chambers Dictionary entry for 'fetish'.) Later Freud would adopt this term to describe the spurious, surrogate object of desire, an object of obsessive fixation. Marx's adoption of the term is linked with all of these uses. In his theory too, the commodity becomes the object of our fixation, an object

· Chapter 8 ·
The Flâneur's Gaze and the Dialectical Representation of London:
Using Woolf's "Street Haunting" as an Example

which we endow with a mystical charm (Haslett 246).

The 'magical charm' of a visual object or a commodity comes from the satisfaction of the ownership, not from the object itself. In other words, the 'spirit' or the aura of a visual object is given by its owner / beholder / gazer. The term 'fetishism' indicates ritual function of a commodity in terms of social practices. The term 'fetishism' reminds us the symbolic level of a commodity—myth, charm, and aura.

A consumer or a receiver of the commodity is fixed by the charm of the commodity— an indulgence of the 'mystical charm' of the commodity. The consumer or the receiver indulges him or herself in the 'charm'—the 'ownership' of the commodity. The 'charm' of the commodity indicates a relationship between individuals. According to Marx, when a material becomes a commodity, its value is transformed, as from wood to a table. This point indicates that the 'charm' and the mysterious element of a commodity come from 'the act of exchange' (Marx 83) and the exchange value of the commodity in the context of social practice. In the economic level, the use value is the 'purpose' (Marx 84) of creating a commodity.

People create commodities because of the 'need'. According to Marx's definition, the exchange value of a commodity reveals a social relation between a consumer and a producer, using money to exchange a commodity. 'Commodity fetishism', claimed Marx, 'is in the world of commodities with the products of men's hands. This I call the Fetishism which attaches itself to the products of labour, so soon as they are produced as commodities, and which is therefore inseparable from the production of commodities' (Marx 83). A world of commodity reveals 'the monetary system' (Marx 93) behind it, which maintains the operation of capitalism. The monetary system is what Marx called an 'illusion'—the ideology, which constructs social relation. It is an illusion, because it is ideological.

However, I suggest that commodity fetishism, in the symbolic level, reinforces the sense of 'ownership'—a relationship among the consumer, the receiver, the beholder and the gazer of the commodity. I argue that the 'charm' and the mysterious element

· Chapter 8 ·
The Flâneur's Gaze and the Dialectical Representation of London:
Using Woolf's "Street Haunting" as an Example

of the commodity come from the 'satisfaction' of ownership—the 'having value' (Marx 84) of a commodity. The sense of 'ownership' brings satisfaction to the consumer via the act of consumption. This satisfaction creates even more desires of consumption and the 'charm' of commodity via advertisement. This sense of ownership maintains the mode of exchange (via money) in the context of capitalist metropolis. The sense of 'ownership' of a consumer reinforces the "Fetish character" (Marx 93)—the harm and the mysterious element of a commodity.

In 'Street Haunting: A London Adventure', the beginning of the text indicates the importance of the sense of "possession", of 'ownership', as

No one perhaps has ever felt passionately toward a lead pencil. But there are circumstances in which it can become supremely desirable to possess one; moments when we are set upon having an object, a purpose, an excuse for walking halfway across London between tea and dinner (Woolf 480).

The 'lead pencil' has two meanings. Firstly, a lead pencil is a commodity, which has been made by materials such as wood and 'a soft, heavy, ductile bluish-grey mental' (Soanes and Stevenson 994). Secondly, a 'lead' pencil symbolizes a 'leading writer', whose literary production is the best in his or her own field and the context of social consumption. A commodity 'pencil' indicates the production of another commodity, a book, via physical and psychological labours of an author / producer.

The 'desire of consumption' is a 'pleasant' motivation for a walk on the street of London. The desire of consumption is "the greatest pleasure of town life in winter" (Woolf 480). According to the text, we can see that to 'own' a lead pencil is a pleasant motivation to the narrator. The sense of ownership gives the narrator a 'wish-image'—an ideological illusion—he or she will write a book, and it will be the best seller.

The narrator steps out of the house and walks into the cityscape 'on a fine evening between four and six' (Woolf 481). This narrator is like a 'foxhunter' with an observational vision of the flâneur. Apart from visual objects, this narrator also

· Chapter 8 ·
The Flâneur's Gaze and the Dialectical Representation of London:
Using Woolf's "Street Haunting" as an Example

hunts sensations and impressions on the street of London. The narrator steps out of the private sphere 'the solitude of one's own room', and walks into a public sphere—the 'society', the network of social relations. Between the 'steps'—'out of house' and 'into the society', the consciousness and the inner gaze of the narrator is wondering around the private sphere—'[f]or there we sit surrounded by objects which perpetually express the oddity of our own temperaments and enforce the memories of our own experience (Woolf 481)'. The phrase 'our own' has been repeated twice. This indicates the importance of the sense of ownership, in terms of the relationship between the owner / beholder / gazer and the visual object. The 'house' is a private sphere, a sacred place, where the narrator collects visual objects and commodities one likes. The house or room is also a symbol of another private sphere—one's own consciousness.

The inner gaze of the narrator sees an object in the house—the blue and white china bowl on the mantelpiece while walking on the street. The mantelpiece is the chancel, and the blue and white china bowl is the mysterious, charming commodity, on which the particular 'moment'' of personal experience has been fixed and connected with a form of 'memory':

> the vines laced about among the pillars and the stars white in the sky. The moment was stabilized, stamped like a coin indelibly, among a million that slipped by imperceptibly. [...]. All this Italy, the windy morning, the vines laced about the pillars, the Englishman and the secrets of his soul—rise up in a cloud from the china bowl on the mantelpiece" (Woolf 481).

To 'possess' the visual object or the commodity ensures the freshness of the memory—as long as the blue and white china bowl has been possessed by the narrator, the narrator can always look at it and think about the past. The blue and white china bowl is a visual object, a commodity for the narrator to fix the inner gaze and memory. Or, the narrator can play with the image of this visual object via the inner gaze, in order to bring an

· Chapter 8 ·
The Flâneur's Gaze and the Dialectical Representation of London:
Using Woolf's "Street Haunting" as an Example

unforgettable moment back to the present. Here, the fetishism of commodity is actually a fetishism of an unforgettable 'moment' of the past. The blue and white china bowl is the commodity, the 'medium' between the 'inner gaze' and 'the memory'—the sinister old woman, the innkeeper and his wife, the courtyard, the vines, the stars, Italy, the Englishman, the secrets of his soul and a cup of coffee—the 'moment'.

The imaginary landscape is a combination of present visual objects of London, personal experiences and memory:

[h]ow beautiful a London street is then, with its islands of light, and its long groves of darkness, and on one side of it perhaps some tree-sprinkled, grass-grown space where night is folding herself to sleep naturally and, as one passes the iron railing, one hears those little cracklings and stirrings of leaf and twig which seem to suppose the silence of the fields all around them, an owl hooting, and far away the rattle of a train in the valley (Woolf 482).

The creation of imagery is in the core self the operation of consciousness / the inward gaze. In this imagery, London has been represented as the Italian countryside. This representation is a mixture of real London visual objects (such as lamps) and the narrator's memory. The imaginary London is based on ideological London. The narrator presses personal memory on the 'ideological' London the 'social' London with the passing crowd. In this imaginary landscape, London becomes a silent alley, where people can hear 'the cracking and stirring of leaf and twig'. Lamps look like stars. The 'night' is like a goddess, who is sleeping on trees and on the grass. This imaginary London is aesthetic, sensational and romantic. The imaginary landscape is a re-production of imagination, memory and present visual objects. This imaginary landscape is an 'impression', which is opposite to the real London a 'market'. It is a synthesis of vision, the operation of consciousness and memory.

It is delightful when the narrator goes back home to 'feel the old possessions' (Woolf 491). Those commodities and visual objects bring 'satisfaction'—a sense of ownership. In the private

· Chapter 8 ·
The Flâneur's Gaze and the Dialectical Representation of London:
Using Woolf's "Street Haunting" as an Example

sphere, one is fixed by commodity fetishism—the 'old prejudices' (Woolf 491). 'And here', claims the narrator, 'let us examine it tenderly, let us touch it with reverence—is the only spoil we have retrieved from the treasures of the city, a lead pencil'.

The flâneur's walk in the cityscape has its own rhetoric. This walking rhetoric, as a social practice, reveals a dual vision—a way of seeing through the surface of a city. Also, the walking rhetoric reveals a way of "being" (Certeau 131) —how a city is lived by the flâneur. The flâneur's vision is a combination of ideology and imagery. This combination is a mode of representation of London in Virginia Woolf's literary text. In 'Street Haunting: A London Adventure', the ideological mode of representation of London is a 'market'. The imaginary landscape of London, on the other hand, is an 'impression' of present visual objects, personal experiences and memory. These dynamic and dialectical powers have been synthesized in literary productions, in the context of social production, social consumption and social practice.

Work Cited

Benjamin, Walter. 'The Paris of the Second Empire in Baudelaire'. *Charles Baudelaire: A Lyric Poet in the Era of High Capitalism*. Trans. Harry Zohn. London: NLB, 1973.

Eagleton, Terry. 'Ideology'. *The Eagleton Reader*. Ed. Stephen Regan. Oxford: Blackwell, 1998.

Habermas, Jürgen. 'The Bourgeois Public Sphere: Idea and Ideology?'. *The Structural Transformation of the Public Sphere; An Inquiry into a Category of Bourgeois Society*. Trans. Thomas Burger. 1989. Cambridge: The MIT Press, 1999.

Haslett, Moyra. 'Cultural and Ideology'. Marxist Literary and Cultural Theories. New York: St. Martin's Press, 2000.

Jay, Martin. 'Lacan, Althusser, and the Specular Subject of ideology'. *Downcast Eyes: the Denigration of Vision in Twentieth-Century French Thought*. 1993. Berkeley: University of California Press, 1994.

· Chapter 8 ·
The Flâneur's Gaze and the Dialectical Representation of London:
Using Woolf's "Street Haunting" as an Example

Marx, Karl. *Capital: Volume 1.* Trans. Samuel Moore and Edward Aveling. Ed. Frederick Engels. London: Lawrence and Wishart, 1996.

Marx, Karl and Frederick Engles. *The German Ideology.* Moscow: Progress, 1968.

Soanes, Catherine and Angus Stevenson, eds. *Oxford Dictionary of English.* Oxford: Oxford University Press, 2003.

Woolf, Virginia. 'Street Haunting: A London Adventure'. *The Essays of Virginia Woolf: Volume IV, 1925-1928.* Ed. Andrew McNeillie. 1925. London: The Hogarth Press, 1994.

A Moment of Joy

語言文學類　PG1200　文學視界63

A Moment of Joy:
Essays on Art, Writing and Life

作　　者 / 林孜郁（Allison Tzu Yu Lin）
責任編輯 / 廖妘甄
圖文排版 / 楊家齊
封面設計 / 秦禎翊

發 行 人 / 宋政坤
法律顧問 / 毛國樑　律師
出版發行 / 秀威資訊科技股份有限公司
　　　　　114台北市內湖區瑞光路76巷65號1樓
　　　　　電話：+886-2-2796-3638　傳真：+886-2-2796-1377
　　　　　http://www.showwe.com.tw
劃撥帳號 / 19563868　戶名：秀威資訊科技股份有限公司
　　　　　讀者服務信箱：service@showwe.com.tw
展售門市 / 國家書店（松江門市）
　　　　　104台北市中山區松江路209號1樓
　　　　　電話：+886-2-2518-0207　傳真：+886-2-2518-0778
網路訂購 / 秀威網路書店：http://www.bodbooks.com.tw
　　　　　國家網路書店：http://www.govbooks.com.tw

2014年09月　BOD一版
定價：200元
版權所有　翻印必究
本書如有缺頁、破損或裝訂錯誤，請寄回更換

讀 者 回 函 卡

感謝您購買本書，為提升服務品質，請填妥以下資料，將讀者回函卡直接寄回或傳真本公司，收到您的寶貴意見後，我們會收藏記錄及檢討，謝謝！
如您需要了解本公司最新出版書目、購書優惠或企劃活動，歡迎您上網查詢或下載相關資料：http:// www.showwe.com.tw

您購買的書名：_____

出生日期：_____年_____月_____日

學歷：□高中 (含) 以下 　　□大專 　　□研究所 (含) 以上

職業：□製造業 　□金融業 　□資訊業 　□軍警 　□傳播業 　□自由業
　　　□服務業 　□公務員 　□教職 　　□學生 　□家管 　　□其它____

購書地點：□網路書店 　□實體書店 　□書展 　□郵購 　□贈閱 　□其他

您從何得知本書的消息？

　□網路書店 　□實體書店 　□網路搜尋 　□電子報 　□書訊 　□雜誌
　□傳播媒體 　□親友推薦 　□網站推薦 　□部落格 　□其他_____

您對本書的評價：(請填代號　1.非常滿意　2.滿意　3.尚可　4.再改進)
　封面設計____　版面編排____　內容____　文／譯筆____　價格____

讀完書後您覺得：

　□很有收穫 　□有收穫 　□收穫不多 　□沒收穫

對我們的建議：_____

_____

_____

_____

11466
台北市內湖區瑞光路 76 巷 65 號 1 樓

秀威資訊科技股份有限公司 　　收

BOD 數位出版事業部

....

（請沿線對折寄回，謝謝！）

姓　　名：＿＿＿＿＿＿＿＿＿　　年齡：＿＿＿＿＿　性別：□女　□男

郵遞區號：□□□□□

地　　址：＿＿＿＿＿＿＿＿＿＿＿＿＿＿＿＿＿＿＿＿

聯絡電話：(日) ＿＿＿＿＿＿＿＿＿　(夜) ＿＿＿＿＿＿＿＿＿

E-mail：＿＿＿＿＿＿＿＿＿＿＿＿＿＿＿＿＿＿＿＿